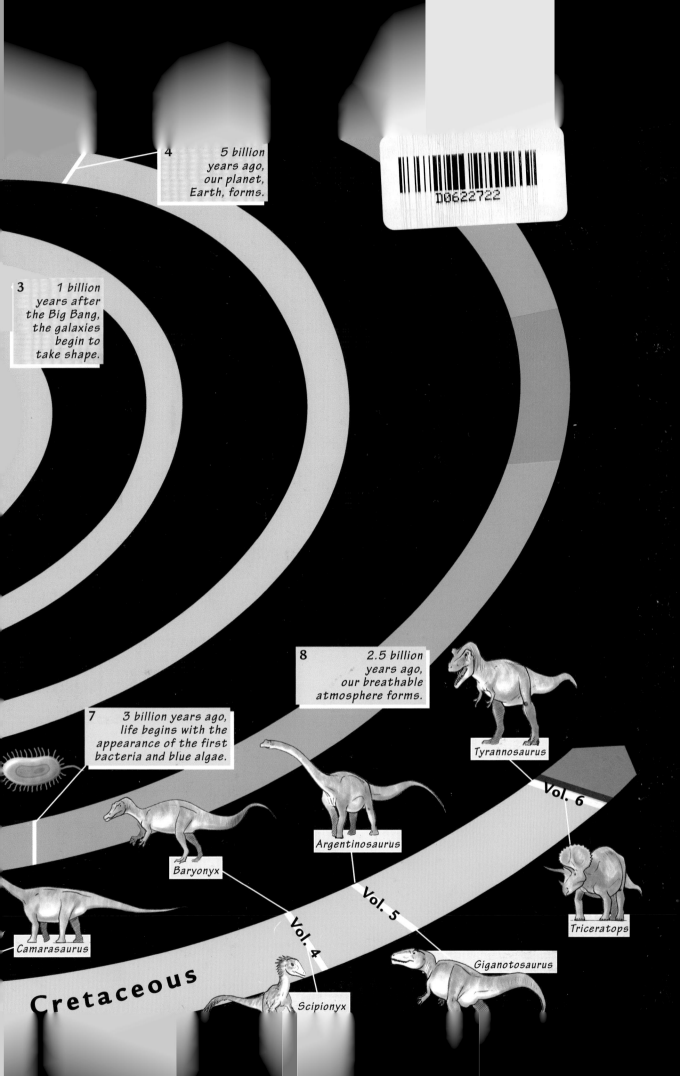

4 5 billion years ago, our planet, Earth, forms.

3 1 billion years after the Big Bang, the galaxies begin to take shape.

8 2.5 billion years ago, our breathable atmosphere forms.

7 3 billion years ago, life begins with the appearance of the first bacteria and blue algae.

Tyrannosaurus

Argentinosaurus

Vol. 6

Baryonyx

Triceratops

Vol. 5

Camarasaurus

Vol. 4

Giganotosaurus

Cretaceous

Scipionyx

# CONTENTS

First published in the United States of America in 2008 by Abbeville Press, 137 Varick Street, New York, NY 10013

First published in Italy in 2008 by Editoriale Jaca Book S.p.A., via Frua 11, 20146 Milano

First edition
10 9 8 7 6 5 4 3 2 1

Library of Congress Cataloging-in-Publication Data
Bacchin, Matteo.
[Delitto. English]
A Jurassic mystery : Archaeopteryx / drawings and story, Matteo Bacchin ; essays and story, Marco Signore ; translated from the Italian by Marguerite Shore.
p. cm. — (Dinosaurs)
Originally published: Il Delitto : Giurassico : Impararono a Volare. Milano : Editoriale Jaca Book, 2008.
ISBN 978-0-7892-0979-5 (hardcover : alk. paper) 1. Archaeopteryx—Juvenile literature. 2. Dinosaurs—Juvenile literature. 3. Paleontology—Jurassic. I. Signore, Marco. II. Title. III. Title: Archaeopteryx.

QE872.A8B33 2008
560'.1766—dc22

2008007614

For bulk and premium sales and for text adoption procedures, write to Customer Service Manager, Abbeville Press, 137 Varick Street, New York, NY 10013, or call 1-800-ARTBOOK.

Visit Abbeville Press online at www.abbeville.com.

For the English-language edition: David Fabricant, editor; Ashley Benning, copy editor; Austin Allen, production editor; Louise Kurtz, production manager; Robert Weisberg, composition; Misha Beletsky, cover design and typography.

# Foreword
## By Mark Norell

One of the most common questions I get is, how does an animal become a fossil? Fossilization is a rare event, and never more so than with early birds like the *Archaeopteryx* whose story is detailed in the pages that follow. In fact, the early history of birds is so poorly known that you could fit every specimen of Mesozoic bird ever collected into my office cabinets. Why is this? Fossilization requires a string of unlikely coincidences. First, the dead animal needs to be buried before the depredations of scavengers and decomposition reduce its body and skeleton to their elemental and molecular components. Obviously this occurs with greater frequency in some environments than in others. Arid savannahs make great fossils. Anyone who has traveled in these areas knows that they are typified by years-old skeletons. Rain forests are the exact opposite. Decomposition starts at death (even before in some cases). I have seen dead birds on the forest floor as I hiked one way and then returned a few hours later to find only a few scattered feathers. Consequently, we know much more about savannah animals than the richly diverse inhabitants of tropical forests. Size is also a factor. Large animals decompose more slowly than small ones. Their bones are tougher. So you can imagine just how difficult it is for a small animal with delicate bones to become a fossil.

That is what makes fossil localities like Solnhofen, where *Archaeopteryx* is found, so special. These specimens preserved not only hard, bony parts but the consummate defining feature of birds—feathers. And these feathers belonged to an animal that also had teeth and a long tail, an animal that was and continues to be a perfect example of a transitional chimera. For the first 150 years of the study of bird evolution, *Archaeopteryx* specimens were looked at like oracles because they were the only direct evidence available of the transition from "reptile" to "bird."

Fortunately, *Archaeopteryx* is no longer unique in its relevance to the origins of birds. In the last decade, hundreds of specimens of early birds have emerged from the rocks of the province of Liaoning in northeastern China. Like the *Archaeopteryx* fossils, these specimens preserve the fossil remnants of feathers and display many transitional characteristics. Additional fossils from Liaoning have also revealed that feathers do not define birds at all, and were present in more primitive dinosaurs, even tyrannosaurs. Solnhofen and Liaoning are the only two places that preserve such animals, and without them our understanding of the early history of birds would be much much murkier.

# DINOSAURS

## A JURASSIC MYSTERY

## ARCHAEOPTERYX

Santa Clara County
**LIBRARY**

Renewals:
(800) 471-0991

# A Jurassic Mystery

## ARCHAEOPTERYX

Drawings and story
**MATTEO BACCHIN**

Essays and story
**MARCO SIGNORE**

Translated from the Italian by Marguerite Shore

**ABBEVILLE KIDS**
A Division of Abbeville Publishing Group
New York   London

# IN THIS STORY

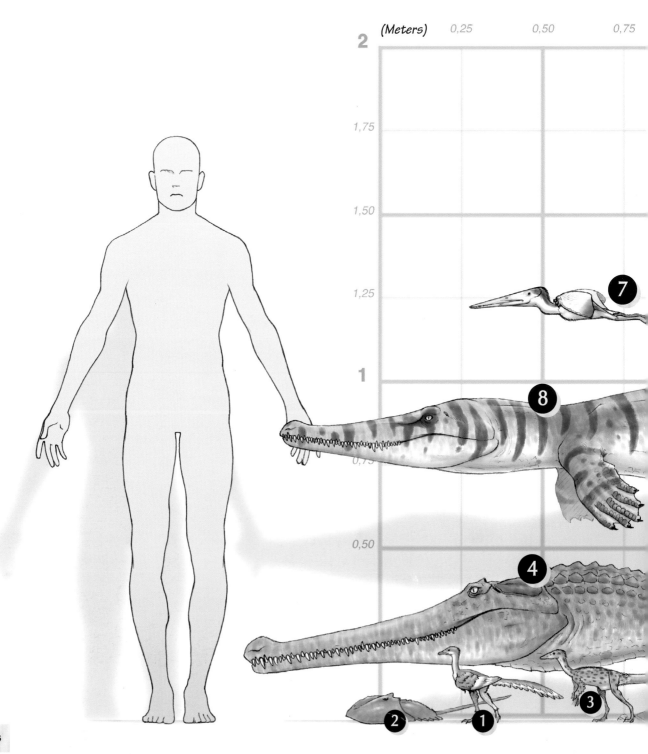

(Meters)  0,25  0,50  0,75

2

1,75

1,50

1,25

1

0,75

0,50

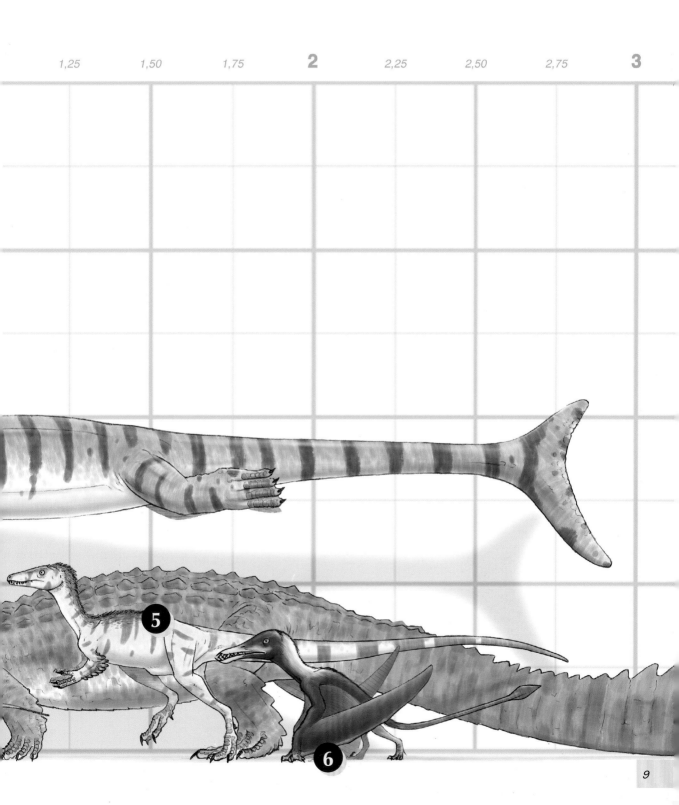

1 Archaeopteryx

2 Horseshoe crab

3 Compsognathus

4 Steneosaurus

5 Juravenator

6 Ramphorhynchus

7 Pterodactylus

8 Metriorhynchus

*See identikit on page 40*

1,25    1,50    1,75    **2**    2,25    2,50    2,75    **3**

# THE NARRATOR

ALLOW ME TO INTRODUCE MYSELF ONCE AGAIN:
I AM A SUN. A YELLOW SUN.

NOT THE LARGEST OR THE BRIGHTEST, AND NOT EVEN THE
FIRSTBORN SON OF THE INFINITE MOTHER UNIVERSE;
AS I HAVE ALREADY TOLD YOU, I AM STILL YOUNG COMPARED
TO OTHER SUNS, WHETHER NEARBY OR DISTANT.
BUT THIS DOESN'T MEAN I HAVEN'T SEEN A LOT,
FOR COMPARED TO MANY OF MY BRETHREN, I AM VERY
FORTUNATE: I AM NOT ALONE IN THIS SMALL DOMAIN
OF MINE.

DIFFERENT WORLDS HAVE FORMED AROUND ME, AND
IN THE TIME I HAVE BEEN GRANTED THUS FAR, I HAVE
WITNESSED MANY DIFFERENT LIVES. IT IS PRECISELY
ONE OF THESE EXCEPTIONAL LIVES THAT I AM GOING
TO TELL YOU ABOUT NOW.

MY STORY TAKES PLACE IN PERHAPS THE MOST
SPECTACULAR AND THRIVING PERIOD THAT THE EARTH
HAS EVER KNOWN, THE LOST MEMORY OF WHICH YOU
HUMANS HAVE DISCOVERED IN ROCK AMONG THE
ROCKS—MOMENTS CAPTURED IN STONE, BEARING
WITNESS TO THAT BYGONE ERA AND TO THE BEINGS
THAT LIVED THEN.

THE EONS HAVE TURNED THESE BEINGS INTO MUTE STONES AND HAVE EMPTIED THEIR CHESTS OF BREATH AND WARMTH, BUT I BRING YOU TESTIMONY OF THEIR ANCESTRAL TIME—A TIME BEFORE THE PYRAMIDS, BEFORE THE GODS, LONG BEFORE THE ERA OF MAN WAS EVEN IMAGINED, AND EVEN BEFORE THE MOST ANCIENT MEMORY OF THE WHALES. THEY WERE THE UNCONTESTED RULERS OF THIS TIME, CONQUERING EVERY CORNER OF THE EARTH AND ASSUMING THE WIDEST VARIETY OF SHAPES. THEY SEEMED INVINCIBLE, AND YET A MYSTERIOUS FATE TRANSFORMED THEM INTO A LEGEND.

SO ALLOW ME TO CONTINUE WITH MY STORY.

I HAVE TOLD YOU ABOUT THE LONG JOURNEY AT THE TIME OF THE NEW TRACKS, WHEN A LONG-NECKED FEMALE WITH SKY-COLORED EYES, ALONG WITH OTHERS LIKE HER, FACED THE BLAZING DESERT, SHARP-EDGED MOUNTAINS, AND HUNGRY PREDATORS, THEREBY COMPLETING ONE OF THE INNUMERABLE RINGS THAT MAKE UP THE INFINITE SPIRAL OF LIFE.

NOW THAT I HAVE REMINDED YOU HOW THESE BEINGS WALKED THE EARTH, HOW THEY WERE BORN, HUNTED, MATED, MIGRATED AND DIED, I WILL ALSO TELL YOU HOW THEY LEARNED TO FLY, PROPELLING THEMSELVES THROUGH THE SKIES WITH ONLY THE HELP OF THEIR DELICATE FEATHERS.

I WILL TELL YOU
ABOUT...
THE
DINOSAURS

# 2 A JURASSIC MYSTERY

IN THE SHALLOW WATERS OF THE LAGOON, THE ERA OF ASCENT IS ENDING.

A SWIMMING CROCODILE SLIDES SILENTLY THROUGH THE TRANQUIL WATER:

IT IS HUNTING FISH.

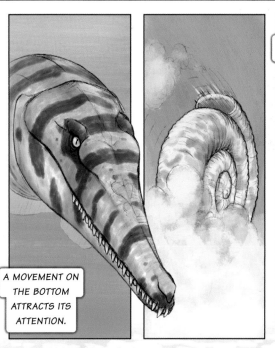

A MOVEMENT ON THE BOTTOM ATTRACTS ITS ATTENTION.

NOTHING APPETIZING...

BUT SOMETHING IS LYING NEARBY, IN THE LIGHT SAND.

THE REPTILE LINGERS TO STUDY THE BODY, SOMETHING NEVER SEEN BEFORE, SO FOREIGN TO HIS LIQUID REALM.

MY SECOND STORY TAKES PLACE IN A REGION THAT, MANY MILLIONS OF YEARS AGO, WAS TRODDEN UPON BY THOSE TRAVELERS I TOLD YOU ABOUT EARLIER.

THE SEA INVADED THIS LAND,

NO LONGER HARSH COASTS, TALL MOUNTAINS, AND ARID DESERTS,

BUT A WARM LAGOON WITH PURE WHITE BEACHES, INHABITED BY MYRIADS OF CREATURES.

PTEROSAURS, CROCODILES, DINOSAURS: THESE PLACES OVERFLOW WITH LIFE.

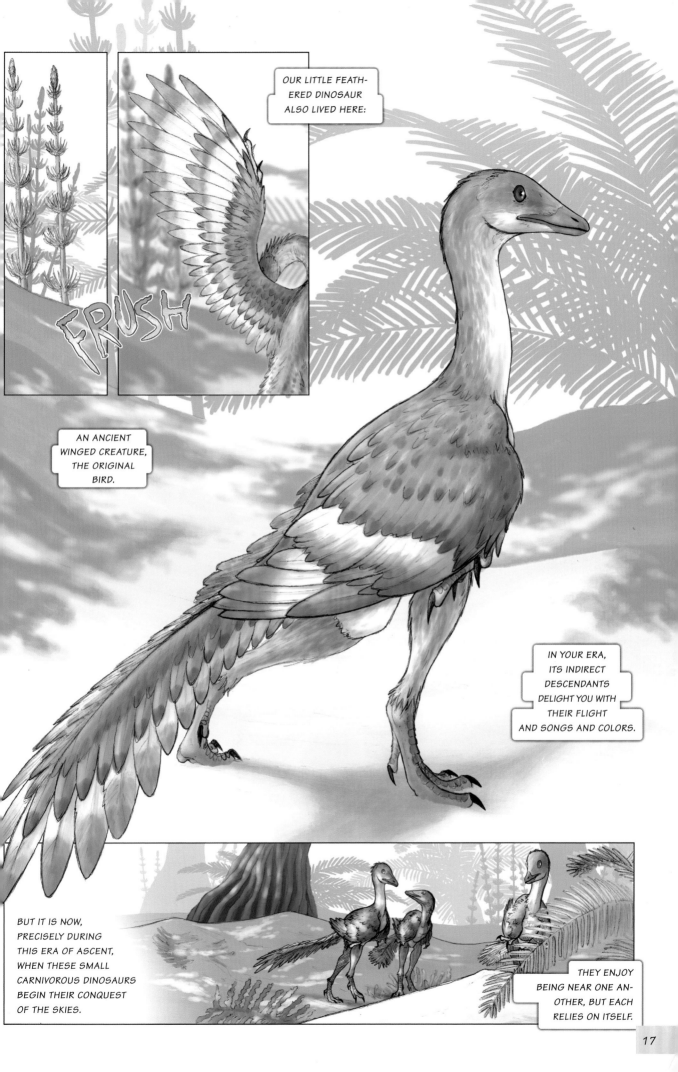

OUR LITTLE FEATH-
ERED DINOSAUR
ALSO LIVED HERE:

FRUSH

AN ANCIENT
WINGED CREATURE,
THE ORIGINAL
BIRD.

IN YOUR ERA,
ITS INDIRECT
DESCENDANTS
DELIGHT YOU WITH
THEIR FLIGHT
AND SONGS AND COLORS.

BUT IT IS NOW,
PRECISELY DURING
THIS ERA OF ASCENT,
WHEN THESE SMALL
CARNIVOROUS DINOSAURS
BEGIN THEIR CONQUEST
OF THE SKIES.

THEY ENJOY
BEING NEAR ONE AN-
OTHER, BUT EACH
RELIES ON ITSELF.

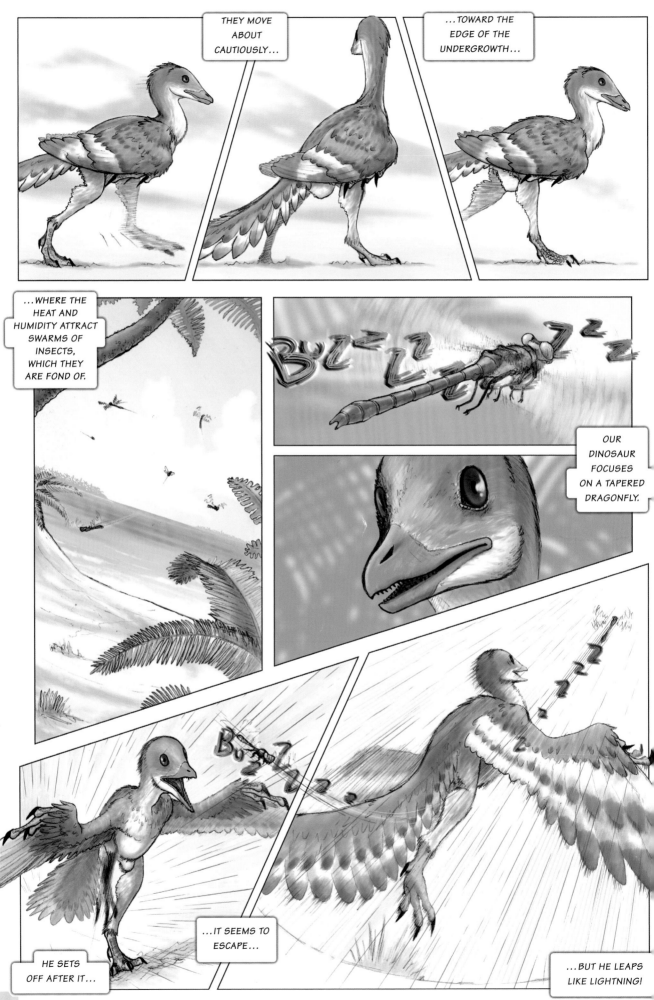

S FEATHERS VIBRATE, SPARKLING AND TRANSLUCENT, IN THE AFTERNOON SUN.

HIS MUSCLES TENSE.

ZIP!

FOR A LONG INSTANT, OUR WINGED ONE REMAINS SUSPENDED IN THE AIR.

CATCH!

WHEN THE DINOSAUR ELEGANTLY FALLS BACK TO EARTH,

THE SUCCULENT INSECT IS HELD FIRMLY WITHIN HIS SHARP CLAWS.

THEN, TILTING HIS HEAD...

...HE MAKES SURE THAT EVERYTHING AROUND HIM IS IN ORDER; HE DOESN'T BEGIN TO EAT UNTIL HE IS CALM.

TAP

BZ!

MEANWHILE A FEMALE, PERHAPS ALREADY SATED, HAS MOVED TO THE EDGE OF THE SHORE.

WASH

WASH

CROUCHING, SHE SPREADS HER WINGS, AS IF TO CAPTURE EVERY RAY OF THE AFTERNOON LIGHT...

...WHILE PTEROSAURS TRACE TRAJECTORIES OVER THE SEA...

KWEEK

KWEEK

KWEEK

KWEEK

KWEEK

CATCH!

...IN STEEP NOSE-DIVES FOR FISH, DARING SWOOPS FOR INSECTS ON THE WATER'S SURFACE.

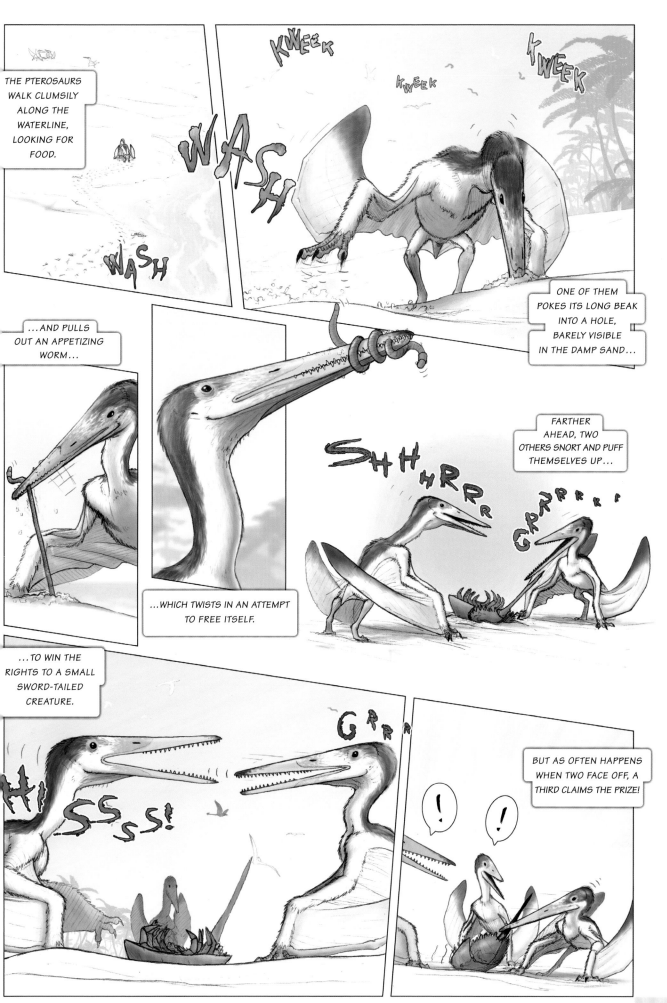

OUR LITTLE DINOSAUR HAS FINISHED HIS MEAL.

IT IS TIME TO GROOM: HE RUFFLES AND SMOOTHS HIS FEATHERS WITH SKILL.

SCRATCH

SCRATCH

THERE IS ALSO TIME FOR A SCRATCH,

BEFORE HE SETS OFF AGAIN TOWARD THE SHADOWY INTERIOR OF THE ISLAND.

!!!

CRAKLE

AFTER A FEW STEPS, A NOISE MAKES HIM FREEZE.

HE'S PETRIFIED, EVERY SINGLE NERVE OF HIS BODY STRAINING TO LOCATE THE POSSIBLE THREAT...

FEAR! A LIGHTNING LEAP!

OUR WINGED ONE HURLS HIMSELF TOWARD A TREE, TOWARD SALVATION!

A MOMENT LATER THE SAND EXPLODES!

THE PREDATOR CRASHES WHERE OUR DINOSAUR HAD JUST BEEN.

THUD!

THE HUNTER HAS LEAPED WITH SO MUCH FORCE THAT IT LOSES ITS BALANCE.

THE SMALLEST HESITATION HAS LED TO FAILURE.

IT GETS UP, HISSING.

HHHHHHHHH

SHAKE

THE NIMBLE PREDATOR SHAKES THE SAND OFF ITS BACK...

SHAKE

IT IS FURIOUS TO HAVE MISSED ITS PREY.

SNORT!

...AND LOOKS UPWARD WITH A GRUNT OF DISAPPOINTMENT.

OUR WINGED ONE HAS TAKEN REFUGE IN THE FOLIAGE, JUST IN TIME.

THE PREDATOR SNIFFS AROUND THE TRUNK.

FOR A FEW MOMENTS, IT STUDIES HOW OUR CREATURE ESCAPED...

...BUT, UNFORTUNATELY FOR THE PREDATOR, IT IS NOT CAPABLE OF CLIMBING UP TO REACH HIM.

A FINAL SNARL OF CONTEMPT DIRECTED AT HIS PREY UP ABOVE...

...AND THEN, DISAPPOINTED BUT NOT DEFEATED,

IT RETURNS TO THE DENSE UNDERGROWTH.

QUIET HAS RETURNED.

LIFE IS HARD, EVEN FOR PREDATORS, WHO OFTEN DO NOT CATCH THE HOPED-FOR MEAL.

OUR WINGED ONE POKES HIS SAPPHIRE-COLORED HEAD FROM HIS REFUGE.

HE HAS AVOIDED DANGER, BUT IS STILL FRIGHTENED.

AFTER A WHILE, THE LITTLE DINOSAUR GOES OUT AS FAR AS THE BRANCH WILL SUPPORT HIM, MAKING IT SHAKE.

THEN HE LETS HIMSELF FALL INTO THE VOID.

FLIP

...TRANSFORMING THE DINOSAUR INTO A BIRD, TRANSFORMING THE DREAM OF GLIDING THROUGH THE AIR INTO A POETIC REALITY OF ELEGANT AND ENERGETIC MOVEMENTS.

BUT WHEN HE OPENS HIS FRONT PAWS AS FAR AS POSSIBLE IN AN ATHLETIC GESTURE, THEY BECOME WINGS, AND HIS FALL TURNS INTO FLIGHT...

HE SLIDES GRACEFULLY
THROUGH THE AIR,
MOVING WITH A SINGLE
BEAT OF HIS WINGS
TOWARD ANOTHER TREE.

IT DOESN'T SEEM
VERY ADVISABLE
TO WALK RIGHT NOW!

FLAP

HE
ALIGHTS ON A
FAVORITE BRANCH,

FRUSH

AND
HIS WINGS TURN
BACK INTO PAWS
TO GRIP IT.

HE
SMOOTHS
HIS
FEATHERS.

HE DOES
THIS OFTEN;
IT IS VITAL
TO KEEP
THEM CLEAN AND
IN WORKING
ORDER.

THE DAY IS
ENDING...

...OUR WINGED ONE
WILL SLEEP IN
THE SAFETY
OF THIS TREE.

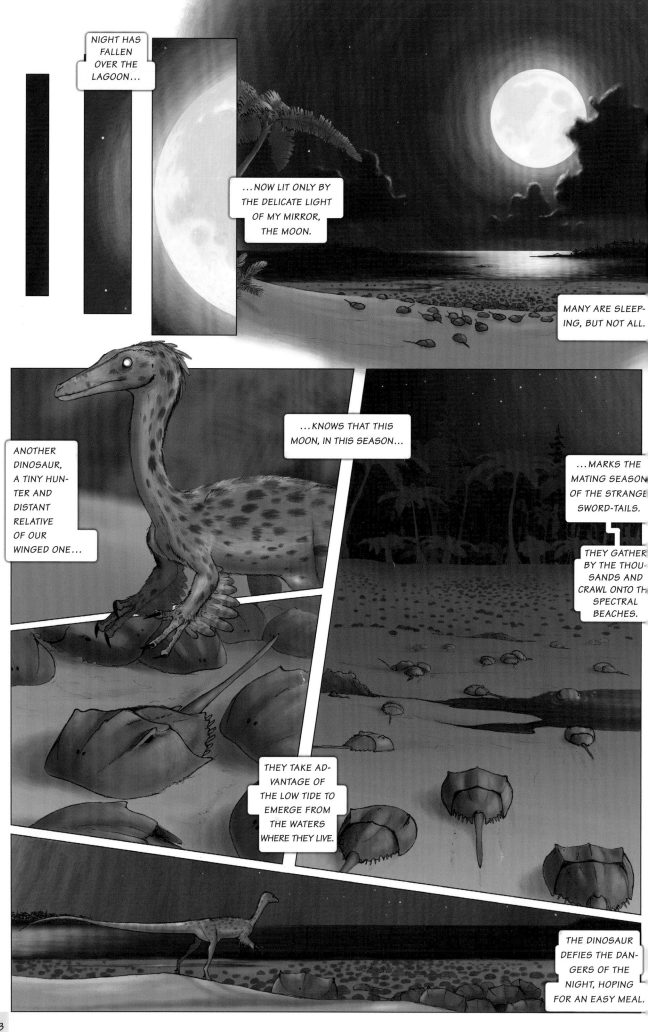

NIGHT HAS FALLEN OVER THE LAGOON...

...NOW LIT ONLY BY THE DELICATE LIGHT OF MY MIRROR, THE MOON.

MANY ARE SLEEPING, BUT NOT ALL.

ANOTHER DINOSAUR, A TINY HUNTER AND DISTANT RELATIVE OF OUR WINGED ONE...

...KNOWS THAT THIS MOON, IN THIS SEASON...

...MARKS THE MATING SEASON OF THE STRANGE SWORD-TAILS.

THEY GATHER BY THE THOU-SANDS AND CRAWL ONTO THE SPECTRAL BEACHES.

THEY TAKE AD-VANTAGE OF THE LOW TIDE TO EMERGE FROM THE WATERS WHERE THEY LIVE.

THE DINOSAUR DEFIES THE DAN-GERS OF THE NIGHT, HOPING FOR AN EASY MEAL.

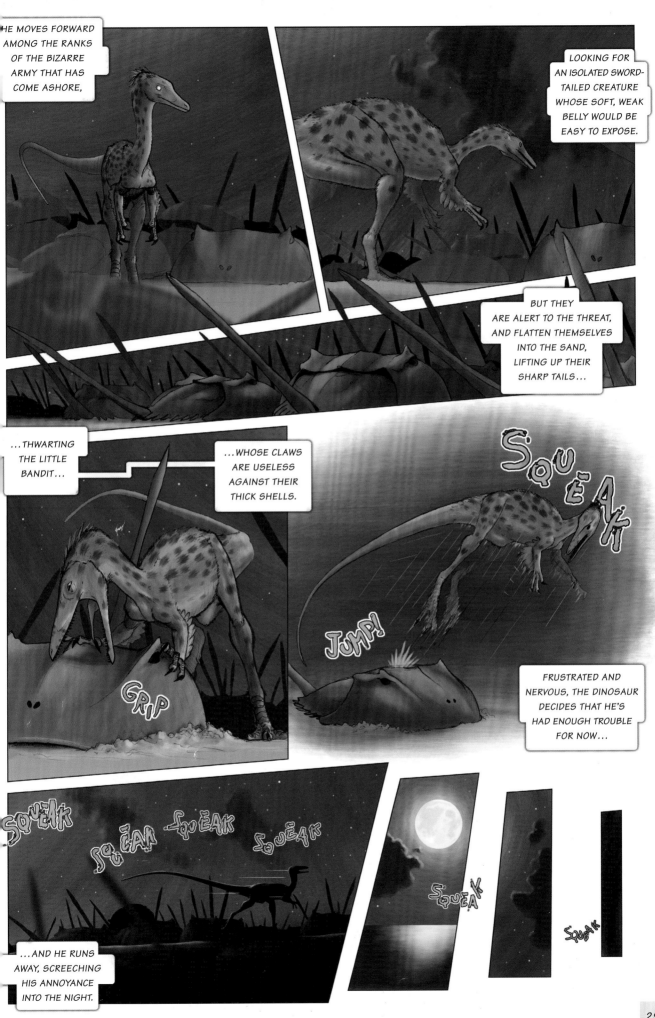

AT DAWN, THE LAST ARMORED CREATURES LINGER ON THE BEACH.

THE LAGOON IS SLOWLY AWAKENING BUT SOMEONE IS ALREADY HARD AT WORK.

LAST NIGHT'S DINOSAUR HAS REAPPEARED WITH SOME ACCOMPLICES, PERHAPS TO AVENGE HIS POOR SHOWING.

CHIRP CHIRP CHIRP CHIRP

SECURE IN THEIR NUMBERS, THEY SQUEAK EXCITEDLY...

CHIRP

CHIRP

...AND SURROUND THE OBJECT OF THEIR DESIRE.

SQUEAK

THEY SCRATCH, BITE, AND FIGHT...

...BUT THE ARMORED CREATURE, HOWEVER SOLITARY...

SQUEAK!

CHIRP

CHIRP

...IS TRULY INVULNERABLE!

WHEN THE QUARTET OF LITTLE HOOLIGANS BECOME TIRED OF FIGHTING THE THICK ARMOR OF THE PATIENT SWORD-TAIL, THEY WILL PROBABLY GO IN SEARCH OF THE EGGS LAID BY THE THRONG OF SIMILAR CREATURES DURING THE NIGHT. PERHAPS IT WILL BE A MORE MEAGER MEAL, BUT CERTAINLY EASIER TO OBTAIN!

THIS IS ALSO THE HOUR WHEN OUR WINGED ONE AWAKENS;

HE SHAKES HIS DROWSY HEAD, SPREADS HIS WINGS, AND ONCE AGAIN CLEANS HIS FEATHERS.

KWEEK!

SHAKE

SHAKE

KWEEK

KWEEK

KWEEK

EEK

THE AIR IS FILLED AGAIN WITH THE SHRILL CRIES OF PTEROSAURS, ENGAGED IN THEIR ENDLESS SEARCH FOR FOOD...

KWEEK

TWEEK

FRUSSSHHHHHHH

...HEATS UP WITH THE COMING OF THE MORNING LIGHT.

...WHILE THE WHITE SAND OF EVERY SMALL ISLAND...

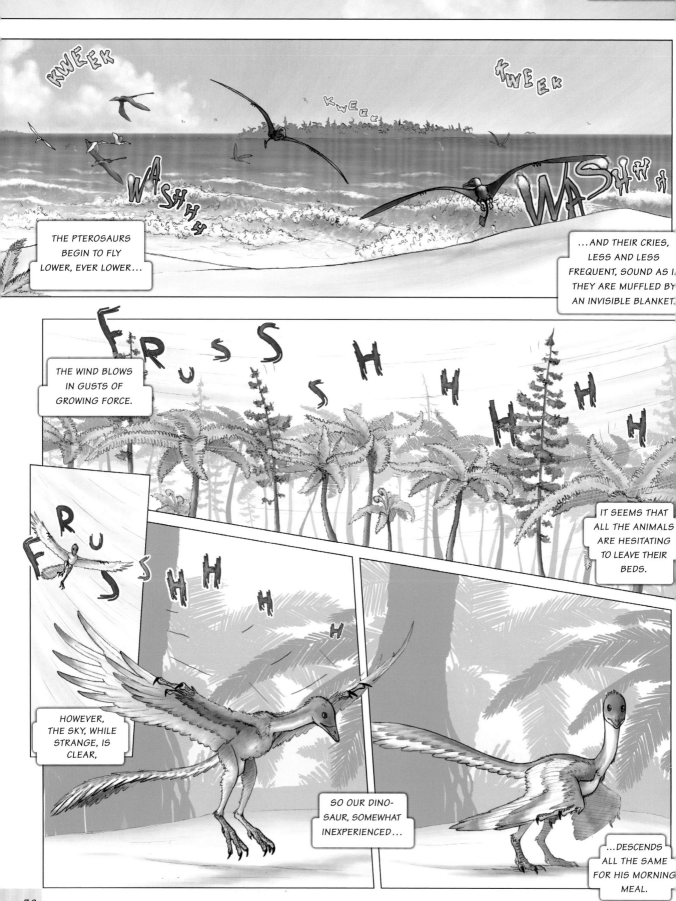

BUT TODAY THE ATMOSPHERE IS DIFFERENT.

KWEEK

KWEEK

KWEEK

KWEEK

WASHHH

WASHHH

THE PTEROSAURS BEGIN TO FLY LOWER, EVER LOWER...

...AND THEIR CRIES, LESS AND LESS FREQUENT, SOUND AS IF THEY ARE MUFFLED BY AN INVISIBLE BLANKET.

FRUSSHHHHH

THE WIND BLOWS IN GUSTS OF GROWING FORCE.

IT SEEMS THAT ALL THE ANIMALS ARE HESITATING TO LEAVE THEIR BEDS.

FRUSSHHHH

HOWEVER, THE SKY, WHILE STRANGE, IS CLEAR,

SO OUR DINO-SAUR, SOMEWHAT INEXPERIENCED...

...DESCENDS ALL THE SAME FOR HIS MORNING MEAL.

MOVING ALONG THE SHORE, PERHAPS OUR CREATURE DISTURBS SOMEONE'S MORNING, BECAUSE...

A YOUNG CROCODILE LEAPS OUT, HISSING WITH HOSTILITY!

SURPRISED, OUR WINGED ONE DOES NOT FLEE BUT PUFFS HIMSELF UP AND SPOUTS AS MUCH RAGE AS HE CAN MUSTER, HOPING HE WILL APPEAR DANGEROUS IN THE EYES OF THE AGGRESSOR.

FOR A LONG MOMENT, THE TWO ANIMALS FACE OFF.

THE AMPHIBIOUS REPTILE IS SMALL, BUT ALREADY HAS SUFFICIENT STRENGTH TO KILL THE DINOSAUR WITH A SINGLE BITE.

OUR WINGED ONE SENSES SOME LETHARGY IN THE STILL-COLD CROCODILE, AND IN A FLASH, FLEES FAR FROM THE DANGER.

WASH

NOW THE SKY DARKENS.

THE SOUTHERN HORIZON SPEWS FORTH ANGRY CLOUDS, PORTENTS OF A STORM; THE SEA SWELLS AND BECOMES MORE AGITATED WITH EVERY MINUTE.

THE WATERS ROAR, BUT OUR WINGED ONE SEEMS TO FACE THEM DOWN IN A TRIAL OF COURAGE...

ROAR!

WASHHH

SPLASHH

...WHILE THE ENTIRE LAGOON IS SUDDENLY THROWN INTO A PREMATURE TWILIGHT.

RRUUMMMMBBLEEEE

THE WIND COVERS THE NOISE, BUT THE THUNDER, STILL DISTANT, RESOUNDS, BOUNCING FROM CLOUD TO CLOUD.

THE FIRST DROPS OF RAIN FALL;

THE STORM SETS IN WITH LITTLE WARNING, A COMMON OCCURRENCE IN THIS SEASON.

THE SHOWER BECOMES A DOWNPOUR...

MANY CREATURES HAVE WISELY REMAINED IN THEIR LAIRS IN THE UNDERGROWTH...

...THE DOWNPOUR BECOMES A FLOOD.

RRRUMMMMBBBLEEEE

...OR BENEATH A FALLEN TREE.

TALL FERNS SHELTER THEM SOMEWHAT FROM THE HEAVY DELUGE.

THE WAVES THAT FURIOUSLY LASH THE BEACHES...

...DO NOT SPARE THE REGIONS BELOW THE SEA'S SURFACE FROM UPHEAVALS AND TUMULT.

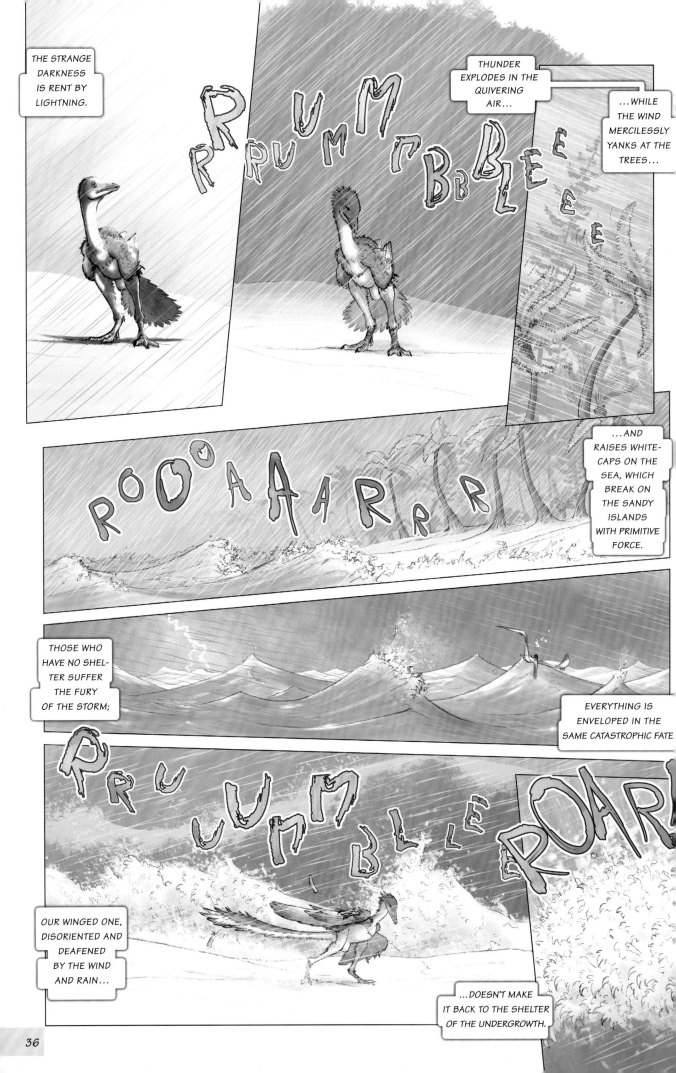

KWEEK

KWEEK

KWEEK

KWEEK

THE SKY IS ONCE AGAIN SERENE.

THE BRIGHT TROPICAL SUMMER RETURNS.

IN THE WATERS OF THE NOW TRANQUIL LAGOON...

...THE LIFELESS, WATERLOGGED BODY OF A FEATHERED ANIMAL ALIEN TO THE SEA...

...SLOWLY BEGINS ITS DESCENT TOWARD THE BOTTOM.

IT IS NOT THE VICTIM OF A CRIME.

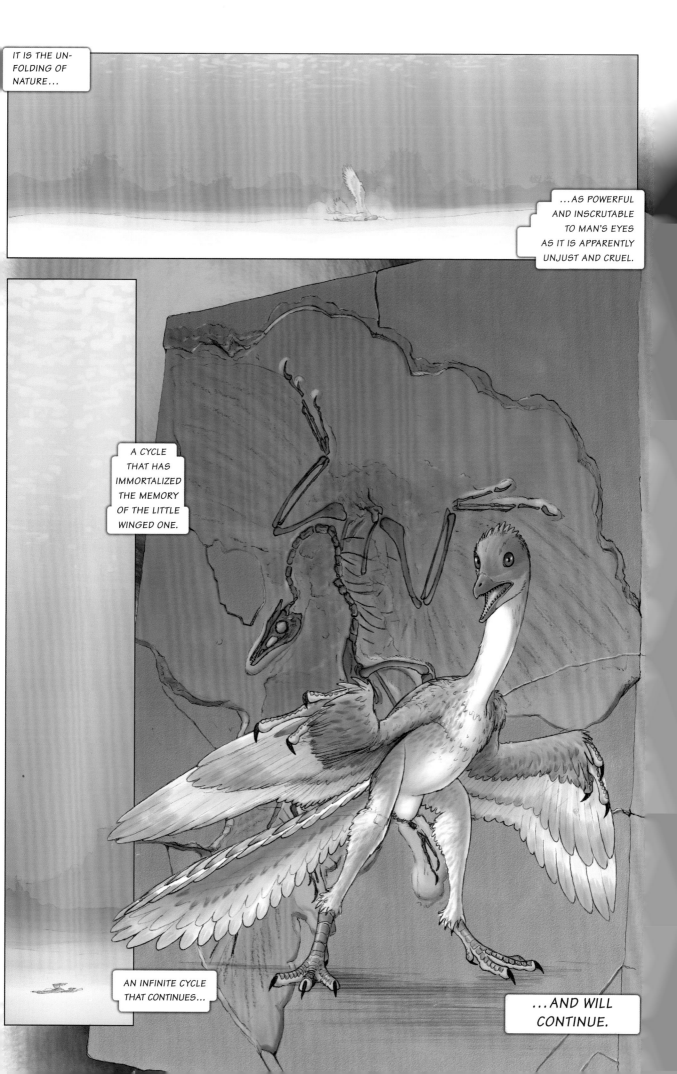

# DINOSAUR EVOLUTION

This diagram of the evolution of the dinosaurs (in which the red lines represent evolutionary branches for which there is fossil evidence) shows the two principal groups (the saurischians and ornithischians) and their evolutionary path through time during the Mesozoic. Among the saurischians (to the right), we can see the evolution of the sauropodomorphs, who were all herbivores and were the largest animals ever to walk the earth. Farther to the right, still among the saurischians, we find the theropods. Among the theropods there quite soon emerges a line characterized by rigid tails (Tetanurae), from which, through the maniraptors, birds (Aves) evolve. The ornithischians (to the left), which were all herbivores, have an equally complicated evolutionary history, which begins with the basic *Pisanosaurus* type but soon splits into Thyreophora ("shield bearers," such as ankylosaurs and stegosaurs) on the one hand, and Genasauria ("lizards with cheeks") on the other. The latter in turn evolve into two principal lines: the marginocephalians, which include ceratopsians, and the euornithopods, which include the most flourishing herbivores of the Mesozoic, the hadrosaurs.

\* This placement within the hierarchy is still under debate.

IDENTIKIT *(see page 8)*

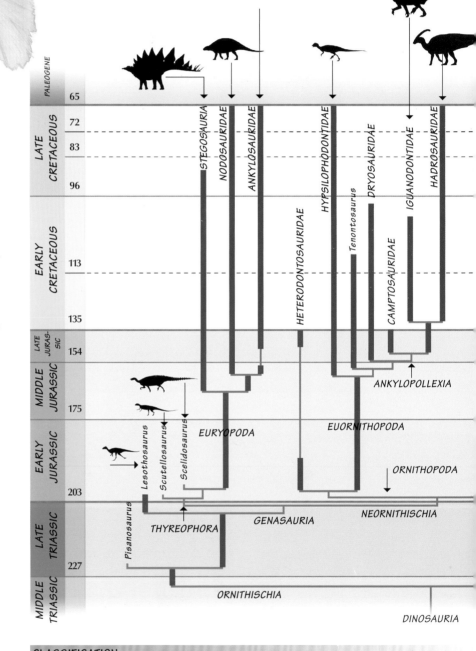

## CLASSIFICATION

| | | |
|---|---|---|
| 1 | Archaeopteryx lithographica | *Saur. > Ther. > Avialae > Archaeopterygid.* |
| 2 | Horseshoe crab (*e.g., the genus* Mesolimulus) | *Arthropoda > Chelicerata > Xiphosura* |
| 3 | Compsognathus longiceps | *Saur. > Ther. > Tetanurae > Coelurosauria* |
| 4 | Steneosaurus (*genus*) | *Mesoeucrocodylia > Thalattosuchia > Steneosauridae* |
| 5 | Juravenator starki | *Saur. > Ther. > Tetanurae > Coelurosauria* |
| 6 | Ramphorhynchus longiceps | *Pterosauria > Rhamphorhynchoidea* |
| 7 | Pterodactylus antiquus | *Pterosauria > Pterodactyloidea* |
| 8 | Metriorhynchus (*genus*) | *Mesoeucrocodylia > Thalattosuchia > Metric* |

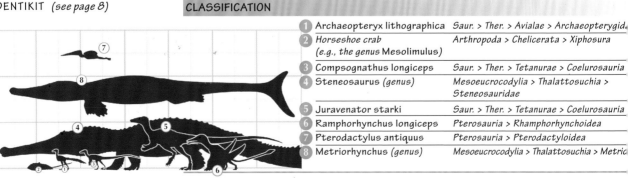

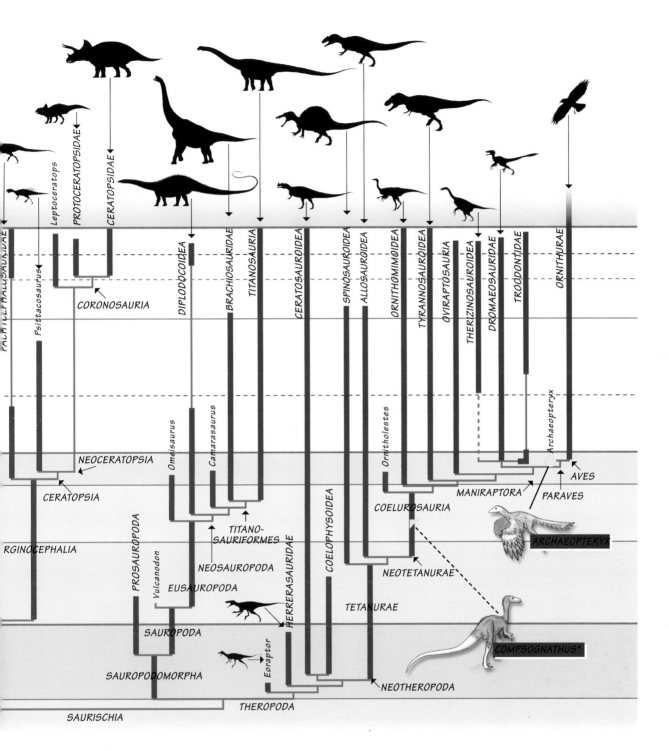

PACHYCEPHALOSAURIDAE

Leptoceratops

PROTOCERATOPSIDAE

CERATOPSIDAE

CORONOSAURIA

Psittacosaurus

DIPLODOCOIDEA

BRACHIOSAURIDAE

TITANOSAURIA

CERATOSAUROIDEA

SPINOSAUROIDEA

ALLOSAUROIDEA

ORNITHOMIMOIDEA

TYRANNOSAUROIDEA

OVIRAPTOSAURIA

THERIZINOSAUROIDEA

DROMAEOSAURIDAE

TROODONTIDAE

ORNITHURAE

Omeisaurus

Camarasaurus

Ornitholestes

Archaeopteryx

NEOCERATOPSIA

CERATOPSIA

AVES

MANIRAPTORA

PARAVES

COELUROSAURIA

ARCHAEOPTERYX

MARGINOCEPHALIA

PROSAUROPODA

Vulcanodon

EUSAUROPODA

NEOSAUROPODA

TITANO-
SAURIFORMES

HERRERASAURIDAE

COELOPHYSOIDEA

NEOTETANURAE

TETANURAE

COMPSOGNATHUS*

SAUROPODA

Eoraptor

SAUROPODOMORPHA

NEOTHEROPODA

THEROPODA

SAURISCHIA

| GTH | HEIGHT | WEIGHT | DIET | PERIOD | TERRITORY |
|---|---|---|---|---|---|
| o 18 inches | up to 10 inches | c. 10 to 14 oz. | predominantly insects | Late Jurassic (Kimmeridgian) | Germany |
| o 24 inches | | up to 8 lbs. | mollusks and other invertebrates | from the Ordovician period of the Paleozoic era to the present day | North America, Europe, Southeast Asia |
| 24 inches | over 10 inches | c. 21 oz. | insects and other small animals | Late Jurassic (Kimmeridgian) | Germany, France |
| o 15 feet | | over 1,100 lbs. | fish and mollusks | from the Early Jurassic to the Late Jurassic | from Asia to North America |
| o 5 feet | 16 inches | 20 to 30 lbs. | small animals | Late Jurassic (Kimmeridgian) | Germany |
| span: up to 5 feet | | unknown | fish, shellfish, mollusks | Late Jurassic (Kimmeridgian) | Germany |
| span: up to 30 inches | | unknown | fish, insects, mollusks | Late Jurassic (Kimmeridgian) | Germany |
| 10 feet | | over 550 lbs. | fish and mollusks | Middle and Late Jurassic | Germany, England |

# THE JURASSIC
## LEARNING TO FLY

# Taphonomy

The protagonist of our story, *Archaeopteryx*, is known for being the first dinosaur with feathers ever to be discovered. Today we know many things about it, but the first question we must answer is, how is it that we know so much? How is it possible that animals that lived 100 million years ago or even earlier have been preserved for all this time and can still give us useful information?

▶ *A fossil of* Aspidorhynchus, *a slender, armored predatory fish that was capable of capturing prey close to the surface, and was equipped with a long rostrum, or snout, a bit like that of a modern needlefish.*

Taphonomy, the branch of paleontology that attempts to answer questions such as this, has a somewhat grim focus, namely the study of what happens to bodies after death. *Taphonomy*, a term that was invented in the twentieth century, comes from the Greek words *taphos* and *nomos*; it means literally "laws of burial." In practice, taphonomy is concerned with the processes that occur from an animal's death until its rediscovery as a fossil. By studying these processes, we can explain how *Archaeopteryx* and its feathers were preserved; also, we can tell how long it floated in the waters of the lagoon after its death, how it ended up on the bottom, how it was buried, and many other things. Sometimes taphonomy also helps us determine the cause of death. It is no accident that taphonomy is widely used by crime scene investigators.

Paleontology studies fossils, and taphonomy explains how these fossils are preserved. We can look at our *Archaeopteryx* as an example, but first we need to take into account certain fundamental facts.

Fossilization is an extremely rare event, one that requires very specific conditions. In fact, organic matter offers little resistance to atmospheric agents and breaks up rapidly, in a series of processes that are grouped under the name necrolysis. Also, organic matter is food, so animal remains immediately become the target of necrophagous (corpse-eating) organisms. Thus, in order for organic matter to be transformed into inorganic matter (which is one of the definitions of fossilization), the remains must be protected.

To be precise, for fossilization to begin, three conditions must be satisfied:

• the organism must have parts that can be fossilized (shells, bones, etc.);

• the remains of the organism must be undisturbed;

• and the remains of the organism must be buried rapidly.

These three conditions occur more frequently in water than on dry land, and the vast majority of fossils known to us are of aquatic organisms or organisms living on land that were transported

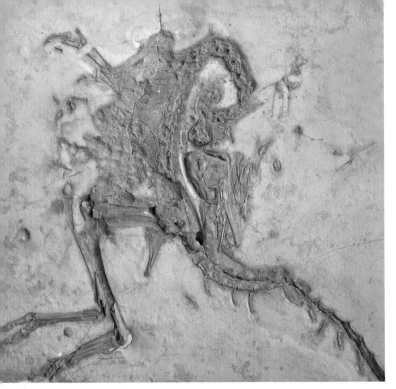

◀ Compsognathus. This small theropod fossil displays some interesting characteristics, such as opisthotonos (the backward curve of the neck). Also, the skeleton is still connected but has a "disorganized" appearance, because decomposition had begun to break up the body before it was covered by sediment.

✱1
page 38
panel 3

✱2
page 15
panel 3

✱3
page 15
panel 4

into the water. There are specific environments in which fossilization is almost impossible, such as forests or mountains, where physical, chemical, and biological agents rapidly break down organic matter, preventing its fossilization.

Once the three conditions are satisfied, it is possible that the remains will become fossilized, provided that the sediments in which they are buried are not swept away by a storm or, once **lithified**, do not undergo **metamorphic processes** (such as high heat or pressure).

But for the purpose of our discussion, let's suppose, as in our story, that the remains of *Archaeopteryx* make it into a lagoon, such as the one that became the fossil bed in Solnhofen, Germany. What happens at this point?

The body is transported by the water, and sooner or later it sinks ✱1. It rests on the bottom and for some reason is not attacked by other animals (for example, the area where it sinks may have little oxygen and thus no other forms of life). Sediment soon covers the body ✱2, and even if some soft tissues are destroyed through putrefaction (decomposition by bacteria), others remain. Time passes, further sediment accumulates, and its weight triggers the processes of lithification. The remains buried within the sediment also undergo transformations. The spaces left in the bones by the disappearance of cells fill up with minerals and expand, hastening the precipitation of new minerals. With time, much of the original material of the bone—if not all of it—is replaced by minerals. Also, the bones may buckle and change their shape due to the weight of the sediment above.

The geological history of Earth teaches us that rocks rarely remain in place, and so **tectonic movements** may push upward what was the bottom of an ancient sea, forming a hill. Rain, wind, landslides, and even the action of plants may then shatter the rocks and expose the remains of our *Archaeopteryx*, which in the meantime have been "replaced" by minerals ✱3.

By chance, a paleontologist or a fossil enthusiast may pass by and notice a bone poking out of the ground. At this point excavations begin, and the fossil is brought to light.

▲ The limestone quarry at Solnhofen, as it looked in the early twentieth century. Solnhofen was quite well known for the quality of its limestone, and the incredible fossils it contained were discovered almost by chance.

Very often, however, paleontologists are not involved, and the fossil is discovered purely by chance, which is precisely what happened at Solnhofen. Later we shall see that the limestone found in this deposit has many uses and has been extracted since Roman times.

The great majority of important paleontological discoveries have been made in this way; and if we consider rocks positioned in inaccessible places (such as Antarctica, for example), we get an idea of how many fossils still wait to be found. Of course, many others have been lost because people have overlooked them or because atmospheric agents have destroyed them.

But taphonomy goes beyond what we have described. For example, why is the head of *Archaeopteryx* bent backward? Since the 1930s, studies carried out on the cadavers of modern animals have revealed that certain processes during decomposition lead to the tightening of the neck

tendons, pulling the head back. This condition, which can be observed in a great many fossils, is known as *opisthotonos*, and it shows us that a cadaver was buried after the processes of decomposition had already started. Also, the fact that the skeleton is almost intact shows that the body remained undisturbed and that it did not float for very long. There are other *Archaeopteryx* fossils that preserve only scant remains, which indicates that the cadaver was exposed to necrophages and atmospheric agents for a much longer time. In many cases, it is even possible to figure out the environmental conditions around the body at the moment of its burial. In other words, the taphonomist truly is a paleontological crime scene investigator. Without taphonomic studies, fossil remains would tell us little and would be simply objects to be collected, almost without scientific value. This is why every serious excavation requires careful taphonomic studies.

▼ One of the best-preserved fish from the Solnhofen deposit. It is possible to make out even the individual rays of its smallest fins.

▼ One of the latest discoveries in the Solnhofen area is this Juravenator, a theropod armed with sharp teeth and sturdy claws, probably the largest predatory dinosaur in the area during the Jurassic.

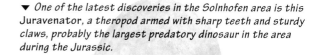

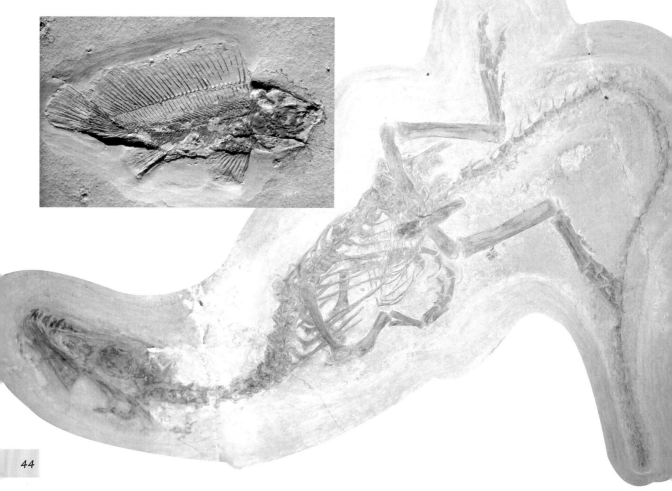

# The Jurassic

The second period of the Mesozoic era, the Jurassic, takes its name from the Jura mountain chain in France. The Jurassic was a period of change and great evolution in flora and fauna, including dinosaurs. In our story we see only a very small part of what we know about this period, yet it is an extremely important part, one that includes almost all the principal types of animals that lived on the planet at the time.

During the Jurassic, the supercontinent Pangaea, which we saw take shape at the end of the Paleozoic era, continued to break apart, as it had begun to do at the end of the Triassic. However, for much of the Jurassic, the continents were still joined together. Generally, the division between the two great landmasses, Laurasia (to the north) and Gondwana (to the south), remained valid, although Laurasia was already beginning to break up into many smaller parts.

The climate was variable, with many zones that experienced aridity or strong rainfall on a seasonal basis. We find evidence of these conditions, for example, in coal deposits (which indicate the presence of great accumulations of plants and therefore of a humid climate) or in evaporates (rocks that are formed by the evaporation of moisture and therefore in an arid climate). As far as we can tell, in the southern part of Laurasia, around the

▲ This is how the planet probably looked during the Late Jurassic. The southern continent, Gondwana, was still more or less undivided, but was clearly separated from the northern continent, Laurasia, which, in contrast, was already breaking apart, with the appearance of numerous epicontinental seas. The orange circle indicates the location of Solnhofen.

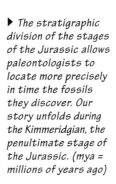

▶ The stratigraphic division of the stages of the Jurassic allows paleontologists to locate more precisely in time the fossils they discover. Our story unfolds during the Kimmeridgian, the penultimate stage of the Jurassic. (mya = millions of years ago)

| | | | |
|---|---|---|---|
| | LATE | Tithonian | 141–135 mya |
| | | Kimmeridgian | 146–141 mya |
| | | Oxfordian | 154–146 mya |
| | MIDDLE | Callovian | 160–154 mya |
| | | Bathonian | 164–160 mya |
| JURASSIC | | Bajocian | 170–164 mya |
| | | Aalenian | 175–170 mya |
| | EARLY | Toarcian | 184–175 mya |
| | | Pliensbachian | 191–184 mya |
| | | Sinemurian | 200–191 mya |
| | | Hettangian | 203–200 mya |

Middle Jurassic, a strongly arid climatic system took hold, which only increased during the remainder of the Jurassic.

Plant life during the Jurassic was still more or less similar to that of the Triassic. There were primitive arboreal conifers and mostly herbaceous ferns. The flora of the Jurassic is fairly well understood, thanks to numerous discoveries in various parts of the world, and that of Solnhofen is no exception, since storms also tore from the ground parts of plants that were then buried in the "lagoon."

In the sea, the Jurassic witnessed numerous changes. After the disappearance of the reef-building bivalves (which you will remember from the previous volume), corals became the greatest reef builders ✻4. And the coral reefs themselves were quite widespread around the globe, thanks to the numerous **epicontinental seas**, such as the one in our story, that occupied vast areas of the planet. Fish were evolving rapidly, with armored forms in clear decline, while marine reptiles were at the height of their splendor.

Ichthyosaurs had now become completely specialized for living in the water and had assumed an optimal shape for swimming rapidly. Deposits in Germany yielded the first evidence that these animals gave birth to living young, rather than laying eggs like other reptiles.

The life of the ichthyosaurs in the Jurassic seas was complicated by the development of new super-predators: plesiosaurs. Descendants of the Triassic nothosaurs we met in the first story, plesiosaurs had now evolved into two distinct lines: the true plesiosaurs, with long necks and small heads; and the pliosaurs, as large as pleasure boats, with short necks, enormous skulls, and teeth over 8 inches long. The size and armament of the pliosaurs indicate that these animals were ferocious and effective predators.

Invertebrates included horseshoe crabs ✻5 and ammonites ✻6; the latter experienced their peak of glory, developing incredible shapes of every size. We know from deposits such as those at Solnhofen that these cephalopods could close their shells with an operculum, or "door," that had two valves known as *aptychi*.

▲ Above, the pliosaur **Pliosaurus**, a ferocious predator over 30 feet long; below, the plesiosaur **Cryptoclydus**, approximately 13 feet long. According to some paleontologists, plesiosaurs fed close to the seabed.

✻4
page 14
panel 5

✻5
page 28
panel 6

✻6
page 14
panel 3

On dry land, plants hosted many insects ✳**7**, among which Orthoptera (crickets and grasshoppers) and Coleoptera (such as beetles) began to appear. Among vertebrates, the herbivores were now dominated by the dinosaurs. At the beginning of the Jurassic, there were still prosauropods, along with basal ornithischians and some residual groups of synapsids, but in the Middle Jurassic, sauropods and thyreophorans became established, along with all the other groups of large herbivores, which we will discuss in greater detail in our next volume.

Crocodiles had now become stabilized in their niche as amphibious predators. In our story, we see them along the coastline of Solnhofen, but some crocodiles, such as the bizarre *Metriorhynchus* ✳**8** and *Steneosaurus* ✳**9**, with its elongated body, began to venture into the sea for longer periods of time, thus evolving into a new type of predator: crocodiles equipped with fins and tails almost like those of fish. We also know about these animals because of deposits like the one in our story. As we mentioned above, however, the Jurassic witnessed the colonization of the last environment still out of range for vertebrates: the air.

While birds were taking their first steps—or rather beginning to spread their wings!—the pterosaurs were the true rulers of the skies. We have seen how the first pterosaurs emerged in the Triassic in Italy. But in the Jurassic, the "lagoons" of Solnhofen accommodated great numbers of these animals, which now were divided into two groups, Rhamphorhynchoidea and Pterodactyloidea. Later we shall discuss pterosaurs in greater detail, but for now let's return to the Jurassic world.

The true lords of the world were now the dinosaurs. Solnhofen is somewhat unusual in that it has yielded evidence not of large dinosaurs, which presumably did not go near coastal areas, but rather of an abundance of small dinosaurs. Among these, one of the most famous is *Compsognathus* ✳**10**, a small animal that was superficially very similar to *Archaeopteryx*, to the point where one of the skeletons of the latter was classified for a long time as *Compsognathus*. This small predator probably lived off invertebrates, lizards, and other animals of modest size, and it surely appreciated the occasional dead sea animal discovered along the coast. *Compsognathus* must, however, have feared the most dangerous predator in Solnhofen, *Juravenator* ✳**11**.

It was only in 2005 that *Juravenator* was first described, although it was discovered many years earlier. The only known fossil of this animal is the complete skeleton of a very young specimen. Completely enclosed within siliceous rock, and thus very difficult to prepare, *Juravenator* finally disclosed its secrets to scientists. From what we can tell, it is a relative of *Compsognathus* and other small dinosaurs (including, presumably, the ancestors of the Italian *Scipionyx*), but the adult *Juravenator* must have been larger than *Compsognathus*. Its jaws were armed with sharp teeth, and the claws of its hands had a decidedly lethal appearance. In our story, *Juravenator* rightly plays the role of the most dangerous animal known from Solnhofen; certainly its appearance must have been dreaded by the small animals that lived along the shoreline, and clearly it could have enjoyed the luxury of feeding off both remains brought in by the tide and living prey.

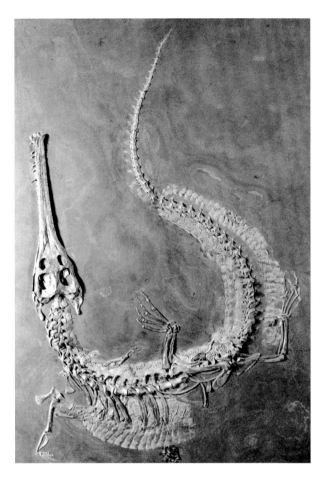

▲ *A large Steneosaurus, an animal that was much more tied to the water than modern crocodiles. Presumably Steneosaurus was piscivorous.*

✳**7**
page 18
panel 5

✳**8**
page 14
panel 5

✳**9**
page 22
panel 5

✳**10**
page 28
panel 5

✳**11**
page 24
panel 4

# The Solnhofen Deposit

Let's return now to our investigation. We have briefly examined the setting of our mystery, the Jurassic. We have gotten to know the possible suspects and also the creatures that were not involved in the "crime" but might have been witnesses to it. And we also have an excellent investigative method, thanks to taphonomy. Now where do we begin in order to understand more about dinosaur life? As in every self-respecting mystery story, let's start with the "scene of the crime": the seabed in Solnhofen, Germany, in the Jurassic.

The lithographic limestone of Solnhofen, from the Late Jurassic, is probably the most famous fossil **Lägerstatte** in the world. Solnhofen is a small village in Bavaria whose quarries of very fine limestone have been known since Roman times and became much more important after Alois Senefelder invented the process of lithography in 1793. The limestone from Solnhofen was clearly the best that could be found for this method of printing, because of its very fine grain and the fact that it could be easily extracted in the sheets needed for press beds. This limestone was also frequently used for construction, so it makes sense that the fossils it contained were noticed rather quickly.

How was the Solnhofen limestone formed? While there have been different theories about how this particular deposit developed, and although scientists do not yet agree exactly on the specifics, we still have gained a rather good understanding of the area's geology.

The area that includes Solnhofen extends for many miles through northwestern Bavaria, and it was part of a low epicontinental Jurassic sea, which at the time extended across much of Europe, from the Paris Basin in France to Vienna in Austria. It would seem that reefs composed of sponges and bacteria frequently formed in this sea. Due to geological changes, these reefs rose up to 160 feet above the surrounding seabed (while remaining beneath the surface of the water, of course), and thus began to isolate large stretches of the surrounding sea bottom. The resulting "lagoons" had less communication with the open sea, and therefore became stagnant. This crisis situation led, in turn, to the decline of the sponge and bacteria reefs, but they managed to persist in certain zones, creating ideal conditions for the sedimentation of a very fine limestone, *Plattenkalk* ("plate limestone"), sometimes known as "lithographic limestone."

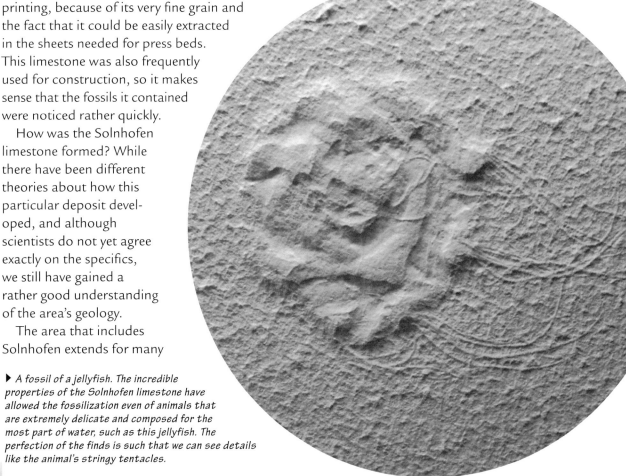

▶ *A fossil of a jellyfish. The incredible properties of the Solnhofen limestone have allowed the fossilization even of animals that are extremely delicate and composed for the most part of water, such as this jellyfish. The perfection of the finds is such that we can see details like the animal's stringy tentacles.*

This type of limestone was formed by sedimentation in very tranquil waters, and taphonomic evidence also indicates an environment that was quite hostile to animals. What probably occurred was that a closed basin, incorrectly called a "lagoon," formed. Because the water had become stagnant, oxygen was likely very scarce at the bottom of this basin, thus slowing down or even preventing the decomposition of bodies, which were often buried by the very fine limestone sediment. Remember that these are two of the three conditions needed for fossils to develop, as we saw earlier. The other condition, the presence of body parts that can become fossilized, is also satisfied: fish and other vertebrates have skeletons of calcium phosphate, and the calcium carbonate shells of mollusks are equally good candidates for fossilization.

However, one question naturally arises: if the conditions in these closed basins were not particularly inviting for animals, why then do we have this abundance of fossils? According to the model that is still most widely accepted, during large seasonal storms animals were transported—dead or alive—into these areas of accumulation ✳12. The storm also stirred up the seabed, and the very fine calcareous mud remained in suspension, while the bodies immediately sank to the bottom. Then the mud resettled and covered everything, like an underwater snowfall.

We should note that this is not the only model that has been proposed to explain the exceptional Solnhofen deposit, and from one day to another, research can change what we know—and to a certain extent, this is true of all paleontology!

Solnhofen is justly famous throughout the world because of the preservation of exceptional fossils, such as the **soft tissues** of animals. Cephalopods and worms are not uncommon in the deposit, but there are fossils that are truly exceptional, such as jellyfish, dragonfly wings, the ink sacs of squid, and phenomenal *Archaeopteryx* feathers. Just think—in one case the ink contained in the fossil of a cephalopod was diluted and then used for writing, and it was still good! However, even for an exceptional deposit like the one we are discussing, such finds are incredible. In fact, what is usually preserved is the impression of parts of an organism, specifically the upper surface of the impression. This type of preservation suggests tranquil conditions, rapid burial, and possibly the growth of a carpet of algae over the bodies. This algal mat, as scholars call it, functions somewhat like a mold that precisely replicates the forms of the remains beneath it. To be precise, it is the mat that is fossilized, not the remains. But in this way we have an almost perfect copy of the upper surface of the remains over which the mat formed.

Another interesting detail about Solnhofen is that some fossils show evidence of dehydration. This led earlier scholars to believe that the organisms preserved in the deposit had been mummified in the open air. Now, however, we know that the dehydration occurred underwater, due to an

▼ In this photo we see a dragonfly. Once again, we cannot help but marvel at the preservation of the fossil in the fine limestone of this ancient seabed; it is even possible to see the veins in the extremely delicate wings.

✳12
page 37
panel 3

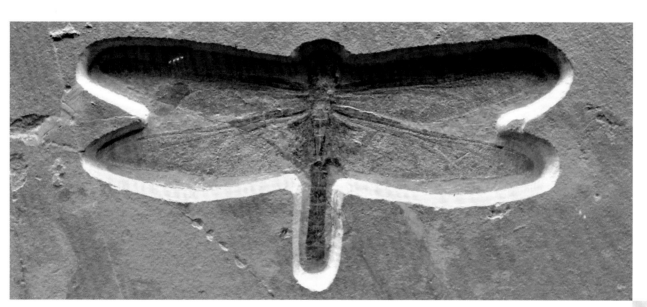

▲ This fossil is quite famous among paleontologists. It is a horseshoe crab, a marine arthropod equipped with armor and a sword-shaped "tail," that became fossilized in its tracks. Paleoichnologists (specialists in fossilized traces of life) call these "tracks of agony," because it is thought that the animal left them in its final moments. This fossil is also unusual because fossil tracks are not generally found together with the animals that have left them, as they are here. It is a decidedly interesting case.

❋13
page 31
panel 4

especially salty environment. In concrete terms, the water contained in the organisms "migrated" outward due to the difference in salt levels between the cadaver and the surrounding water, effectively mimicking open-air mummification.

To summarize, the fossiliferous zones of Solnhofen were closed and hypersaline basins to which organisms were transported, dead or alive, by storms. Even if an organism arrived there alive (which seems to have occurred, to judge, for example, from the so-called "tracks of agony" of certain arthropods), it would soon die; live terrestrial organisms obviously would have expired from drowning. Then the cadavers sank and were deposited on the seabed; decomposition was slowed by the hypersaline solution in which the bodies were submerged, so there was plenty of time for the very fine sediment to be deposited over the remains, allowing fossilization. In some cases, the algal mat we mentioned earlier formed over the cadavers. And this is why we can learn about a great variety of animals, both marine and terrestrial, that lived around these "lagoons." For example, flying insects have been preserved in minute detail. According to some experts, these insects were transported to the sea by storms, were trapped by the wind, and ended up drowning in the water. And the storms also carried off some of the plant cover from the land; in fact, terrestrial plants are well represented in Solnhofen. The vegetation around the basin was not exceptionally luxuriant and did not exceed about 15 feet in height ❋13. Mostly there were shrubs, including large ones, and low plants, which could have sheltered terrestrial life. We also know of many other animals from the dry land around the lagoon, including certain lizards, crocodiles, and, of course, dinosaurs.

In this context, one of the most famous and important animals in paleontology, *Archaeopteryx*, was deposited and preserved. This small theropod even helped Darwin demonstrate his theory of evolution, because its skeleton was discovered precisely during those years of great scientific controversy. But for its descendants, *Archaeopteryx* represents much more. Like a prehistoric Wright brother, this feathered animal embodies the dream of all creatures: flight.

# Flight in Vertebrates

Flying is an undoubted advantage, but it requires an incredible expenditure of energy. Nevertheless, flight has opened up new prospects in evolution ever since its first appearance in the distant Carboniferous period, among insects.

Vertebrates were slow to achieve this "third dimension." The ability to glide, that is, to "passively" travel through the air over more or less brief distances, has evolved numerous times in the history of vertebrates. Think, for example of present-day gliding animals: flying lizards, frogs, and snakes, as well as mammals such as the flying squirrel. However, gliding is not the same as flying. Gliding animals extend a membrane and then use it to "improve" their jumps. We might say that gliding is a sort of "sail-jumping," in which devices are used to prolong the trajectory of the jump. Energy is expended at the beginning of the jump and at the landing, but staying aloft in the air for brief stretches uses up no energy. In any case, gliding provides a degree of freedom—but it is not the same as flying!

Flying, rather, means moving actively through the air. Flying requires a quantity of energy that gliders will never have, as well as specific anatomical adaptations, and usually body structures that are much more specialized than those found in gliding creatures. There is a reason that throughout the history of vertebrates, powered flight has appeared only three times (if you want to include humans, with airplanes, then four times; but humans are cheating, because an airplane is not an anatomical modification). The first vertebrates to fly were probably pterosaurs, which were archosaurs related to dinosaurs; in our story, they occupy the skies above the lagoon. Then come birds, which are really specialized carnivorous dinosaurs; finally, there are mammals, namely, bats. These are the only three cases of active flight known among vertebrates.

An animal that wants to fly must have specific qualifications:

• a lightening of the skeleton, to decrease the weight to be transported;

• the development of a metabolic system that is more efficient under certain conditions, to provide the energy needed for flight;

• thermal insulation, to keep body heat (and thus energy) from being lost during flight;

• wings, to create the series of physical effects that make it possible to lift off from the ground and remain in the air;

• and a sensory system, to govern flight and orient oneself in the air.

We shall discover all these things in our three groups of flying vertebrates—and, strangely enough, in man-made airplanes! Let's look at them again, one by one, and let's also see how man has resolved the same problems using technology.

Flying creatures have the lightest possible skeletons: they either use cartilage in place of bone, or,

▲ *Modern birds, such as this heron, are adapted to life in almost every terrestrial environment, thanks to their ability to fly. However, their wings, feathers, and other characteristics have remained unchanged from those of their earliest ancestors.*

more commonly, have especially light bones. If we observe the skeleton of a bird, we can see that the bones are fragile and nearly hollow. The inner part of the bones is held together by a series of pillars but is otherwise effectively empty. Such bones, associated with the presence of air sacs (that is, spaces full of air), make birds the best flying creatures that have ever developed. In airplanes, the structure is lightened through the use of particular materials (in the biplanes of the early twentieth century, wood and canvas, and in later aircraft, aluminum or light alloys).

During flight, much energy is needed; an efficient breathing system (which in birds is specialized to the highest possible degree) allows the entire body to be nourished with oxygen. Moreover, a substantial diet allows energy to be stored. Large quantities of insects or the seeds of monocotyledons (such as grasses and other flowering plants), which are very high in calories, are among the "fuels" that birds use to fly. Humans use . . . well, they use engines and high-performance fuels. (Just think of the jet engines that power airplanes like the SR-71 Blackbird, capable of traveling more than three times the speed of sound.)

Flight puts the organism in contact with a hostile environment, where temperatures are lower on average than on land. Moreover, the flier's velocity creates an airflow that removes heat from the surface of its body, thereby causing its internal heat to be drawn out. The results for the animal in

question would be disastrous if it weren't for the existence of insulating materials. Pterosaurs and flying mammals are equipped with a hairy covering, while birds have developed the most perfect possible insulation: plumage. That's why coats and comforters are filled with feathers! Pilots must also wear heavy clothing when they fly, or control the climate in their aircraft, as is done on passenger planes.

Of course, a flier must overcome the force of gravity, at least for a brief time, in order to rise up from the surface of the earth. What happens beneath and above a wing is explained by the laws of physics, which lie outside the scope of this book, but it suffices to know that the wings function in such a way that the air itself raises the body up from the ground and keeps it in flight. Have you ever watched a bird in a nosedive (or a dragon in some science fiction film)? Have you noticed that to accelerate it closes its wings, and to slow down it reopens them? The wings are an essential component both for taking off and for landing, as well as for changing speed during flight. The wings also create the physical thrust that enables the animal to move itself through the air (a sort of "swimming in the sky"). Of course, it is obvious that all three groups of flying vertebrates have highly developed wings, and that man-made airplanes also are equipped with wings.

But while moving, it is also important to see where you are going, and for this a system of highly

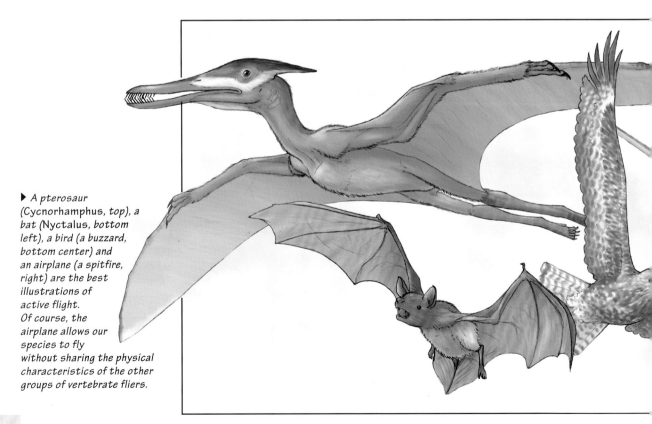

▶ A pterosaur (Cycnorhamphus, top), a bat (Nyctalus, bottom left), a bird (a buzzard, bottom center) and an airplane (a spitfire, right) are the best illustrations of active flight. Of course, the airplane allows our species to fly without sharing the physical characteristics of the other groups of vertebrate fliers.

developed sensors is needed. In fact, the nervous systems of flying animals are very well developed, in order to monitor the entire organism moment by moment, and usually sight is employed as a navigational tool—along with a sort of built-in compass that is present, for example, in migratory birds. Pterosaurs also had highly developed sight, while bats have a system of ultrasonic sonar with which they "see" their surroundings, somewhat like the comic-book superhero Daredevil. The truly unusual fashion in which these marvelous animals see the world may seem strange and almost inconceivable to us . . . but actually, we do the same thing in our modern airplanes, with radar systems and other navigational instruments.

How did flight develop among dinosaurs, from which birds then originated? At the current time, two different theories exist. The first theory sees the origin of flight in **arboreal** animals, which used their ability to glide to increase the range of their movements, while the second theory takes into consideration evidence that flight evolved from running terrestrial animals that used their capacity to "lengthen their jumps," as it were, in order to become more effective in hunting or escaping danger. The first theory, which is less accepted, claims, among other things, that birds and dinosaurs are only distantly related; this is one of the greatest difficulties with the first theory, since it seems that birds actually did evolve from dinosaurs.

However, according to the second theory, the running terrestrial predators were actually dinosaurs. And it would seem that feathers are also found in nonflying carnivorous dinosaurs, as the most recent discoveries in China show. Although the "from the earth up" theory still remains just a theory, and the final word is not yet in, the available evidence points to flight evolving from terrestrial and not arboreal animals.

Feathers were "baggage," as it were, already present among theropods ✳**14**. We know that feathers derive from scales, but we still do not know the reason why they evolved. The most obvious reason is thermal insulation, and yet the Jurassic (and late Triassic) climate was not cold. In short, we still do not have a convincing explanation. We like to think that feathers evolved as a system of communication, as a form of **visual display** for dinosaurs, yet to demonstrate the validity of one theory or another, we will need much more fossil evidence.

Let's return to the Jurassic. At this moment, the pterosaurs began to reach their evolutionary peak, while birds were successfully taking off into active flight. They would soon be able to outclass the pterosaurs, but for now the air was still the realm of the "winged lizards." We will look more closely at these exceptional cousins of the dinosaurs, before moving on to the protagonist of our story, *Archaeopteryx.*

✳14
page 25
panel 3

◀ *Certain things are shared in common by all fliers: wings, rather broad and elongated; a head (or a cockpit in the case of an airplane), for receiving all the signals and data needed for flight; and an aerodynamically shaped body, which presents the least possible resistance to the air.*

# Pterosaurs

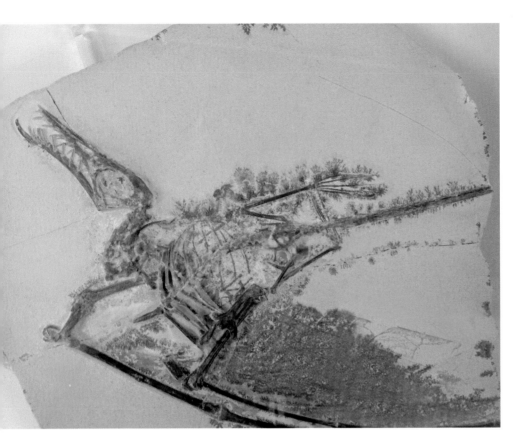

✳15
page 20
panel 4

✳16
page 20
panel 5

✳17
page 21
panel 1

✳18
page 21
panel 3

Pterosaur means "winged reptile," and we have seen in *The Journey* how pterosaurs appeared at the end of the Triassic. We do not know their origins, but we do know that in the Jurassic, pterosaurs underwent a long period of evolution.

Earlier we mentioned that during the Jurassic, two principal groups of pterosaurs existed. On the one hand there were Rhamphorhynchoidea (*Rhamphorhynchus* appears in our story) ✳15, flying animals equipped with sharp and developed teeth and a long tail that presumably acted as a rudder. Representatives of this group were closer to the primitive pterosaurs of the Triassic in Italy. Their teeth were still large and robust, while their skull, however enlarged, did not attain the extremes that we shall see in the Cretaceous among pterodactyls; the long tail was another characteristic that clearly distinguished them from their relatives. (There were two exceptions, both very small pterosaurs with a rounded head and almost no tail, which, however, were clearly rhamphorhynchoids: *Anurognathus* and *Batrachognathus*.) One immediately visible characteristic of rhamphorhynchoids was that the head proceeded directly from the neck, forming a single line.

Pterodactyls, meanwhile, had a very short tail

▲ Rhamphorhynchus *was a relatively primitive pterosaur, clearly piscivorous, and equipped with a long tail that ended in a diamond-shaped flap of skin. Its teeth were few but sharp, like harpoons, allowing it to prey upon slippery creatures such as fish. The specimens from Solnhofen probably belong to several species of* Rhamphorhynchus, *though some scholars believe these are instead examples of a single species at various stages of growth.*

and a much larger skull, equipped with smaller teeth; in this group of pterosaurs, the skull hooked onto the neck at a 90-degree angle, as if it were resting on top of it, rather than forming a continuous line with it. Pterodactyls would be the only creatures to challenge birds for the domination of the skies in the Cretaceous, and they would develop forms with wingspans similar to those of a modern fighter plane, exceeding—if the estimates from some fossils discovered a few years ago prove to be accurate—65 feet. But for now we shall settle for more modest dimensions, such those of the *Pterodactylus* ✳16 in our story. From the traces they have left, we know that these animals were capable not only of flying, but also of walking on four paws ✳17; and presumably they added to their diet, for the most part based on fish, by looking for worms and other animals in the coastal sands ✳18.

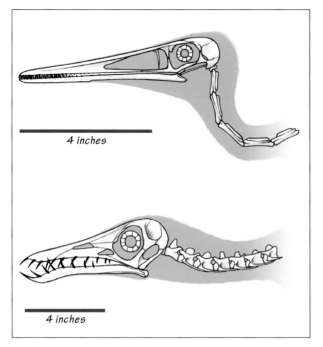

4 inches

4 inches

▲ The skull of Pterodactylus (above) compared to that of Rhamphorhynchus (below). First of all, it is important to note the orientation of the head: in Pterodactylus the head is perpendicular to the neck, while in Rhamphorhynchus it is in line with the neck. The shape of the skull also differs: in Pterodactylus it is more tapered, has smaller teeth, and displays a fusion of the cranial openings behind the eye socket (the antorbital and nasal openings tend to merge). By contrast, in Rhamphorhynchus the skull is more robust, with larger teeth and less pronounced openings.

Scholars are still wondering about many aspects of the ecology of the pterosaurs. For example, we do not know with certainty how these animals took off or landed. It was only recently discovered that they must have had a quadrupedal gait—and not all scholars agree on this point. Where they lived also remains a mystery. All known pterosaurs seem to have been coastal animals, but it is hypothesized that some lived far from the sea, or even among the trees. We still do not know how they could maneuver in such restricted spaces without tearing their wing membranes on branches. Nor have we ever discovered pterosaur fossils that can be located with certainty far from the seas of their time. In short, however well known they are, these ancient flying reptiles are still among the most mysterious creatures of the past.

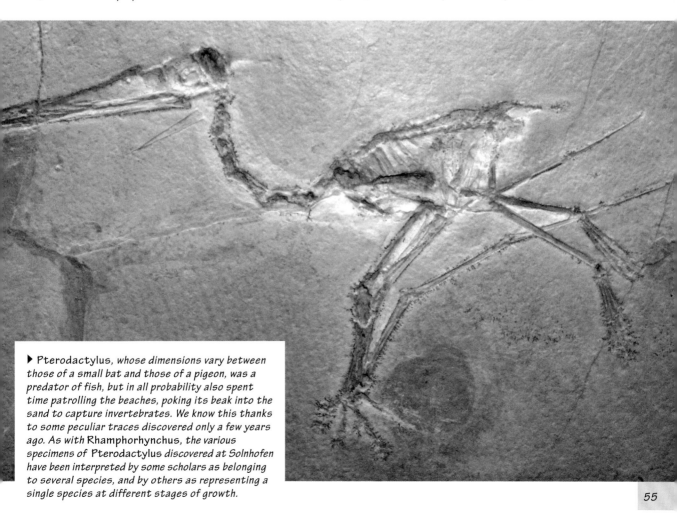

▶ Pterodactylus, whose dimensions vary between those of a small bat and those of a pigeon, was a predator of fish, but in all probability also spent time patrolling the beaches, poking its beak into the sand to capture invertebrates. We know this thanks to some peculiar traces discovered only a few years ago. As with Rhamphorhynchus, the various specimens of Pterodactylus discovered at Solnhofen have been interpreted by some scholars as belonging to several species, and by others as representing a single species at different stages of growth.

# Archaeopteryx

Without a doubt, one of the most celebrated animals of the Jurassic, and one that comes precisely from Solnhofen and the surrounding zones, is *Archaeopteryx*, the protagonist of our story. When it was first described, in 1862, this small creature caused a sensation. In fact, *Archaeopteryx* has characteristics of both a reptile and a bird ✳**19**. Like a reptile, it had teeth, paws with claws, and a long tail, but its feathers clearly make it similar to a bird. The description of the first *Archaeopteryx* was published only two years after Charles Darwin's *On the Origin of Species*, and it was precisely what was required to reinforce the abundant evidence described in the book. Darwin's theory of evolution described the passage from one form of an organism to another through "conjunctive links"; as the link between reptiles and birds, *Archaeopteryx* embodied this concept exactly.

Since that first discovery, many other examples of this animal have been found (at least eleven), and some scholars have even described a new genus based on a famous example of *Archaeopteryx* without feathers (which, because of its structure, was mistaken for *Compsognathus*). Today various scientists support the idea that this specimen belongs to a new genus called *Wellnhoferia*, in honor of the great German paleontologist Peter Wellnhofer.

*Archaeopteryx* is undoubtedly quite an interesting animal. Its most immediately apparent feature is its plumage. The feathers of the limbs and tail of this theropod have been studied in some detail; they are asymmetrical, equipped with barbs and barbules (structures present in the feathers of birds), and they already seem adapted to flight. On the contrary, the plumage of the body has been studied in detail only in one specimen, and thus we know fewer specifics. We do know that much of the animal's body was covered with feathers, but perhaps not the thumb, the lower part of the rear paw, the head, and the neck. And yet according to some scholars, the bareness of these areas in the fossils could be the result of a **taphonomic artifact**. In practical terms, the lack of feathers might be explained by the fact that they had already been detached, due to the start of decomposition, when the animal was buried. In fact, we have preferred to represent *Archaeopteryx* with more complete plumage, both to keep in mind the possibility of this taphonomic artifact and to convey an image that clarifies the relationship between non-avian theropods and birds.

The skeleton of our plumed dinosaur also has mixed characteristics: along with jaws armed with teeth, a long tail, and, according to some scholars, an extremely mobile second toe on its foot (which has been compared to the crescent-shaped talon of the well-known *Velociraptor*), the Solnhofen theropod also had some bone structures typical of

▲ *One of the rare fossils of* Archaeopteryx. *In this case, however, the feathers have not left an imprint.*

✳19
page 17
panel 3

▶ *One of the best-preserved* Archaeopteryx *specimens. We can observe such details as the feathers on the wings and on the long tail; the teeth; the claws on the fingers of the forelimbs; and the neck turned backward in the characteristic opisthotonic posture. We can also clearly see the resemblance between* Archaeopteryx *and* Compsognathus, *both theropods.*

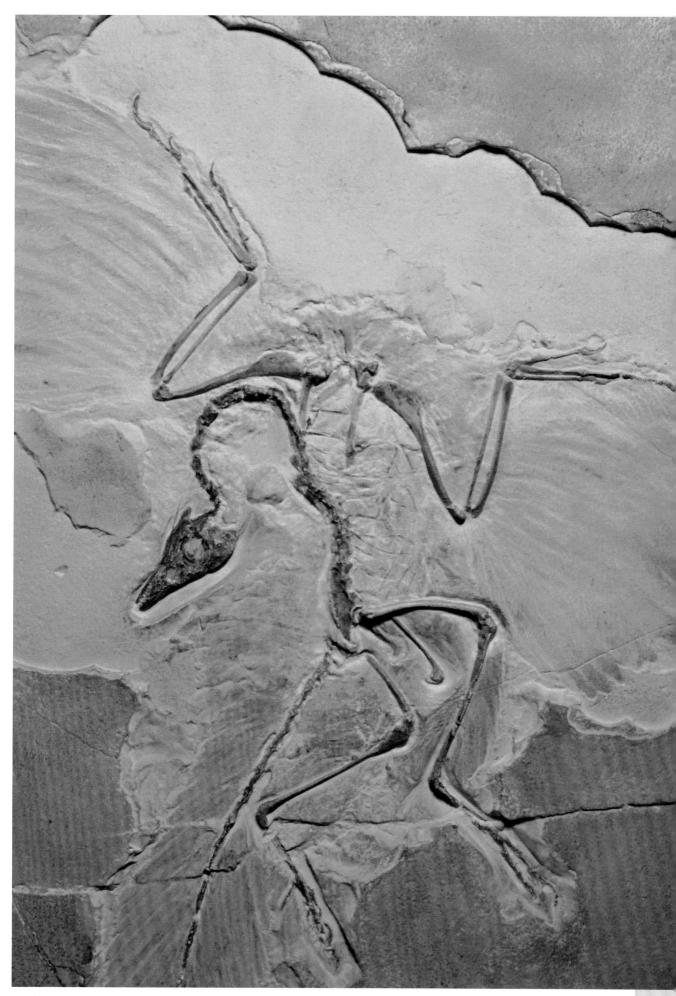

birds, such as a backward-pointing pelvis. As we have seen, this is a mix of characteristics that truly would have pleased Darwin in the most difficult period of his career as a naturalist.

How well did *Archaeopteryx* fly? One paleontologist has come up with a rather evocative simile, comparing *Archaeopteryx* to a "Wright brothers airplane," and modern birds to a Spitfire, that is, a fighter plane. By this, he means that *Archaeopteryx* was not a skilled flier. In fact, the skeleton does not exhibit a keel-shaped and reinforced breastbone to which the flight muscles of the chest could attach. However, the animal's wings and tail are clearly constructed to generate a thrust from the ground upward (thus for flying), and the muscles could have been attached to the powerful furcula, or wishbone, or to the sturdy coracoids of the shoulders; the fact remains that we still do not know if *Archaeopteryx* was a true flier or perhaps a glider capable of traversing greater

than normal distances with a longer and better-structured glide **20**.

But another feature that supports the idea of a flier is the brain of *Archaeopteryx*. Tomographic analysis, which shows three-dimensional images of internal structures, has shown that the brain of this animal is larger on average than those of the dinosaurs, and it has been suggested that it could have accommodated the complex system of sensors that, as we mentioned earlier, is necessary for flight. Along with this, there is the structure of the inner ear, which seems much more like that of modern birds than that of non-avian dinosaurs, making it reasonable to suppose that *Archaeopteryx* had good hearing, and also excellent spatial coordination (another requirement for flight).

Paradoxically, despite the excellent state of preservation of some fossils, we do not know much about the lifestyle of this small carnivore. We know from its skeleton that it was probably a

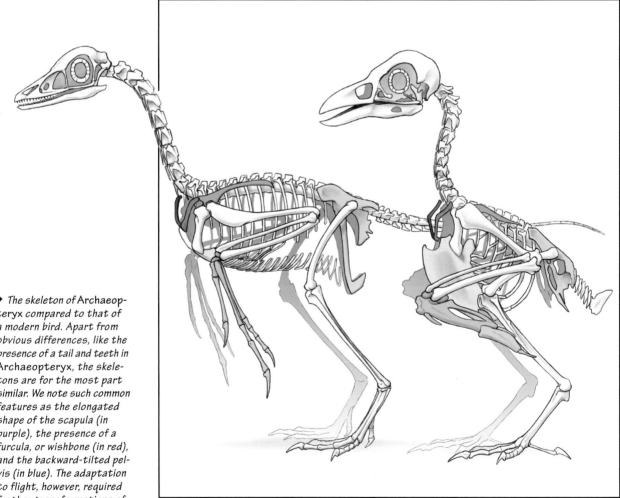

▶ *The skeleton of* Archaeopteryx *compared to that of a modern bird. Apart from obvious differences, like the presence of a tail and teeth in* Archaeopteryx, *the skeletons are for the most part similar. We note such common features as the elongated shape of the scapula (in purple), the presence of a furcula, or wishbone (in red), and the backward-tilted pelvis (in blue). The adaptation to flight, however, required further transformations of the skeleton, and so we see that the sternum, or breastbone (in yellow), of modern birds is much more developed and equipped with a carina, or keel-shaped projection. The forelimbs undergo significant* changes, principally in the hand (carpus in orange, metacarpals in green, phalanges in pink). The fingers are reduced in number and modified in shape and function, and in general the entire forelimb, along with the sternum, is structured to provide thrust in the air.

**20**
page 27
panel 1

predator, because both its claws and its teeth seem adapted to a carnivorous diet. But we do not know if it lived in trees or on the ground; given the type of low vegetation that must have been typical of Solnhofen, *Archaeopteryx* probably could have lived all over. Thus it was likely a generalist, capable of feeding both where the vegetation was most dense, and in open spaces and along the shores of the lagoon. We can imagine *Archaeopteryx* almost as a sort of seagull, except instead of feeding off fish, it hunted terrestrial animals—but if need be, it could patrol the coast, feeding off whatever it found that was edible.

*Archaeopteryx* holds a place of honor in the history of science. This animal clearly demonstrates that theropods were plumed and that birds and dinosaurs are closely related, a fact that is now debated by very few scholars. Indeed, it is one of the most famous fossils in the world, so much so that two scientists from other disciplines who are absolutely ignorant of paleontology (Fred Hoyle, an astronomer, and Lee Spetner, a physicist) wrote a book to demonstrate that the *Archaeopteryx* fossil in the Natural History Museum in London was a fake. Their accusations, brilliantly refuted by English paleontologists, were based on their ignorance about the processes of fossilization and on absurd hypotheses. For example, according to these two scientists, *Archaeopteryx* was created by the great English anatomist Richard Owen to support the ideas published by Darwin. Unfortunately, Owen despised both Darwin and his ideas about evolution!

But certainly the principal "merit" of *Archaeopteryx* is that it is the oldest known bird. The Germans define it perfectly with the term *Urvogel*, which can be translated as "primordial bird" or "original bird." The discovery of new plumed dinosaurs has only confirmed what the various *Archaeopteryx* specimens had already triumphantly announced 150 years ago, namely that the small theropods were equipped with feathers, and that birds evolved from dinosaurs. The first *Archaeopteryx* specimen to be discovered was, in fact, one of its feathers, in 1860; it is interesting to note that this feather, or protofeather as some paleontologists prefer to call it, still has no definite attribution: it was classified at the time as *Archaeopteryx lithographica*, but according to some scientists, it does not resemble any of the feathers discovered on the other *Archaeopteryx* specimens known to science.

And yet only one year later, an almost complete *Archaeopteryx* skeleton was discovered, missing only its head. This fossil, the first true *Urvogel*, is now in the Museum of Natural History in London. Indeed, scientists call it the "London specimen." Every *Archaeopteryx* discovered thus far is distinguished from the others by the name of the place where it is now preserved. The London specimen was described by Richard Owen as *Archaeopteryx macrura* (because he did not believe it belonged to the same species as the feather discovered the previous year), and it is specifically this specimen that Darwin acclaimed (with much relief) as the

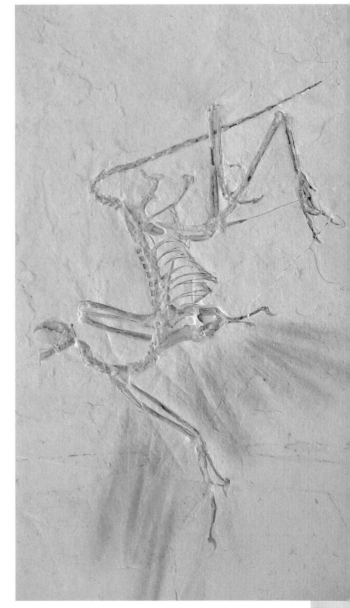

▶ *The skeleton of another species of* Archaeopteryx. *The nearly total lack of feathers (which, however, are visible as impressions in the rock) and the lack of most of the skull are taphonomic artifacts that indicate that the body probably remained exposed in the water for some length of time before sinking and being buried.*

"missing link" between reptiles and birds, and as definitive proof of his model of evolution.

Approximately fifteen years later, a third specimen, now in Berlin, was discovered, this time including the skull. There are two odd things about this specimen: it was given away by its discoverer in exchange for a cow, and today some people think that it is another species and call it *A. siemensii*, in honor of the great industrialist Werner von Siemens, who financed the acquisition of the fossil by the Museum für Naturkunde in Berlin.

Almost all other known *Archaeopteryx* specimens were discovered in the twentieth century, but there is one exception. The specimen preserved at Teylers Museum in Haarlem was discovered in 1855 and thus technically would be the first specimen in chronological order, but because of its poor state of preservation it was classified as *Pterodactylus*. It was not until 1970 that the eminent paleontologist John Ostrom realized this error and reclassified this fossil correctly. Finally, in 2005 a specimen in a private collection was discovered and described. This specimen, which has now

been donated to the Wyoming Dinosaur Center in Thermopolis, Wyoming, has certain anatomical details that were previously unclear in the other specimens. In the Thermopolis specimen, the second toe of the foot is said by some scholars to have a structure almost identical to that of the dromeosaurs, such as *Velociraptor*. At the same time, the first toe of the foot is not opposable, as it is in birds. This detail would greatly limit the arboreal abilities of *Archaeopteryx*, but at the same time it is considered a clear link to other theropods. It should be mentioned that the Thermopolis specimen is sometimes classified as *A. siemensii* as well.

And all this comes from studying a small body discovered in the mud. It is truly a story worthy of the greatest detective films.

However, the Jurassic has only just begun to reveal its surprises, and if in this story we have provided a glimpse into the world of small dinosaurs, our next story will take us to the Morrison Formation in North America, to have a look at the life of some of the largest animals that have ever walked the earth ✳21.

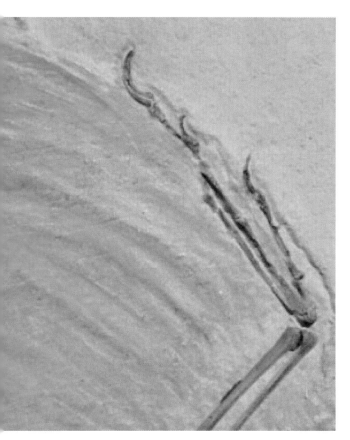

▲ *Detail of an* Archaeopteryx *hand. Note the three elongate fingers, the mobile and rounded wrist, and the feathers covering the arm. In many ways, it is still the hand of a theropod, but we clearly are seeing a very different use of the same structure.*

✳21
*Volume 3*
The Hunting
Pack: Allosaur

# GLOSSARY

**Arboreal:** living in or having to do with trees.

**Epicontinental sea:** a sea that existed in the past within one of today's continents; for example, much of Germany was covered by such a sea (depicted in our story) in the Jurassic period.

**Lägerstatte:** German for "storage place"; a sedimentary deposit containing either very numerous or very well preserved fossils.

**Lithification:** the conversion of a sediment to solid rock by geological processes.

**Metamorphic process:** a process that transforms one type of rock into another type. There are two basic kinds of metamorphism: one caused by high temperature, and one caused by pressure or stress.

*On the Origin of Species:* the book that set forth the modern theory of evolution; written by Charles Darwin and first published on November 24, 1859, in England.

**Precipitation:** the accumulation as a solid of a substance previously dissolved in a medium such as water, due to an increase in that substance's concentration in the medium, or a chemical change.

**Soft tissue:** a part of an organism that is not hard, such as the skin, internal organs, or muscles.

**Taphonomic artifact:** a modification caused in a fossil by a taphonomic process; for example, the lack of feathers in one of the *Archaeopteryx* fossils is a taphonomic artifact.

**Tectonic movement:** a movement of one or more of the large masses of the earth's crust, due to continental drift or local causes, such as the appearance of a hot point beneath the crust; one example is the formation of the Himalayas due to the collision between India and Asia.

**Visual display:** the way some animals "show themselves off"; for example, when a peacock spreads its tail.

## Acknowledgments

For their help and support both direct and indirect, Matteo Bacchin would like to thank (in no particular order) Marco Signore; Luis V. Rey; Eric Buffetaut; Silvio Renesto; Sante Bagnoli; Joshua Volpara; his dear friends Mac, Stefano, Michea, Pierre, and Santino; and everybody at Jurassic Park Italia. But he thanks above all his mother, his father, and Greta, for the unconditional love, support, and feedback that have allowed him to realize this dream.

Marco Signore would like to thank his parents, his family, Marilena, Enrico di Torino, Sara, his Chosen Ones (Claudio, Rino, and Vincenzo), la Compagnia della Rosa e della Spada, Luis V. Rey, and everybody who has believed in him.

# DINOSAURS

## 1  THE JOURNEY: *Plateosaurus*

We follow the path of a great herd of *Plateosaurus* from the sea—populated by ichthyosaurs—through the desert and mountains, to their nesting places. Their trek takes place beneath skies plied by the pterosaur *Eudimorphodon*, and under the watchful eye of the predator *Liliensternus*.

We discover what life was like on our planet during the Triassic period, and how the dinosaurs evolved.

*(In bookstores now)*

## 2  A JURASSIC MYSTERY: *Archaeopteryx*

What killed the colorfully plumed *Archaeopteryx*? Against the backdrop of a great tropical storm, we search for the perpetrator among the animals that populate a Jurassic lagoon, such as the small carnivore *Juravenator*, the pterosaur *Pterodactylus*, crocodiles, and prehistoric fish.

We discover how dinosaurs spread throughout the world in the Jurassic period and learned to fly, and how a paleontologist interprets fossils.

*(In bookstores now)*

## 3  THE HUNTING PACK: *Allosaurus*

We see how life unfolds in a herd of *Allosaurus* led by an enormous and ancient male, as they hunt *Camarasaurus* and the armored *Stegosaurus* in groups, look after their young, and struggle amongst themselves. A young and powerful *Allosaurus* forces its way into the old leader's harem. How will the confrontation end?

We discover one of the most spectacular ecosystems in the history of the Earth: the Morrison Formation in North America.

*(Coming in Spring 2009)*